Mr. Wadd

Theodore Winthrop

(Editor: Burton Egbert Stevenson)

Alpha Editions

This edition published in 2023

ISBN : 9789357954372

Design and Setting By
Alpha Editions
www.alphaedis.com
Email - info@alphaedis.com

Contents

CHAPTER I
A REMARKABLE EPISODE, HITHERTO UNRECORDED, IN THE VOYAGE OF THE "MAYFLOWER"

NAMES must act upon character. Every preceding Waddy, save one short-lived Ira, from the first ancestor, the primal Waddy, cook of the *Mayflower*, had been a type of placid meekness, of mild, humble endurance. During all Boston's material changes, from a petty colony under Winthrop to a great city under General Jackson, and all its spiritual changes from Puritanism to Unitarianism, Boston divines had pointed to the representative Waddy of their epoch as the worthy successor of Moses upon earth—Moses the meekest man, not Moses the stalwart smiter of rocks and irate iconoclast of golden calves.

Why, then, was Ira Waddy, with whom this tale is to concern itself, other than his race? Why had he revolutionised the family history? Why was he a captor, not a captive of Fate? Why was the Waddy name no longer hid from the world in the unfragrant imprisonment and musty gloom of a blind court in Boston, but known and seen and heard of all men, wherever tea-chests and clipper-ships are found, or fire-crackers do pop? Why was Ira Waddy, in all senses, the wholesale man, while every other Waddy had been retail? Brief questions—to be answered not so briefly in this history of his Return.

Yes, the Waddy fortunes had altered. To the small shop, the only patrimony of the Waddy family, went little vulgar boys in days of Salem witchcraft, in days of Dorchester sieges, and after when the Fourth of July began to noise itself abroad as a festival of the largest liberty: on all great festal days when parents and uncles rattled with candy money, and coppers were certain, and on all individual festal days when the unlooked-for copper came, then went brats, Whig and Tory, Federal and Democrat, to the Waddys' shop and bullied largely there. Not only the representative Mr. Waddy did they bully and bargain into pecuniary bewilderment and total loss of profit, but also the representative Mrs. Waddy, a feeble, scrawny dame, whose courage died when she put the fateful question to the representative Mr. Waddy, otherwise never her spouse.

But there was no more bullying about the little shop. In fact, the shop had grown giantly with the fortunes of the name. A row of stately warehouses covered its site, and many other sites where neighbour pride had once looked down upon it. The row was built of granite, without ornament or gaud, enduring as the eternal hills. On its front, cut in solid letters on a gigantic block, were the words

Ginger was sold there in dust-heaps like a Vesuvius, not gingerbread in the amorphous penny idol; aromatic cinnamon by the ceroons of a plundered forest, not by the chewing-stick for dull Sabbath afternoons; tea by the barricade of chests, product of a province, not by the tin shoeful, as the old-time Waddys had sold it for a century before the Tea Party. And Ira Waddy owned these buildings, which he had never seen.

It is not necessary that I should speculate to discover where the traits that distinguished Ira Waddy from his ancestors had their origin. Of this I have accurate information. My wonder is at the delay in a development of character certain to arrive. But late springs bring scorching summers. Fires battened long below hatches gather strength for one swift leap to the main-truck.

Whitegift Waddy, cook of the *Mayflower*, was meek. How he came to be a Puritan, on the *Mayflower*, in its caboose and a cook,—out of his element in religion, in space, in place, and in profession,—I cannot say; these are questions that the Massachusetts Historical Society will probably investigate, now that the Waddys are rich and can hire cooks to give society dinners. At all events, there he was, and there he daily made a porridge for Miles Standish, and there he peppered the same. Now as to pepper in cream tarts there is question; in porridge none: I do not, therefore, blame Miles, peppery himself and loving pepper, for wrath when, one day, a bowl of pepperless insipidity was placed before him. He sent for the cook and thus addressed him:

"Milksop! Thou hast the pepper forgot. I will teach thy caitiff life a lesson. Ho, trencherman! Bring pepper!"

It was brought. He poured it all into the porridge, and, standing by, compelled Waddy to swallow spoonful after spoonful. At the screams of the victim, the Pilgrim Grandfathers, Governor Carver, Father Winslow, and Elder Brewster, rushed from on deck into the cabin and besought the infuriated hero to desist as he valued the life of Mrs. Susanna White, who was soon to add a little Pilgrim to their colony.

"Enough!" said Standish. "The pepper hath entered into his soul."

It had, indeed! Nothing was cooked on the *Mayflower* for six days. On the seventh, Whitegift Waddy re-entered the caboose. He had always been a meek, he was now a crushed man. Yet there seemed to have grown within him, as we sometimes see in those the world has wronged, a quiet confidence in a redressing future.

Pepper, thus implanted in the Waddy nature, seemed to have no effect for generations. It was, however, slowly leavening their lumpishness. It was impelling them to momentary tricks of a strange vivacity. At last, the permeating was accomplished, and our hero, Ira, the first really alive Waddy, was born. I have said the first, but there was another Ira Waddy who, at one period in his brief career, showed a momentary sparkle of the smouldered flame. Of him a word anon, as his fate had to do with the fates of others, strangely interwoven with the fate of his great-nephew and namesake.

CHAPTER II
THE WADDYS OF DULLISH COURT, FROM WHITEGIFT TO OUR HERO

WHILE Governor Winthrop was planning the future city of Boston, he went, one rainy day, to the heights of those hills that give the spot the name of Trimountain. A violent June storm had channelled the hillsides, and strong water-courses filled the valleys. No phenomenon is idle to the observing mind.

"These channels," said the prudent governor, "shall be the streets of our future city."

He then pursued his way downward, slipping along the oozy trails, until he paused at a small pool where several little, muddy rivulets united to form a stagnancy. Here, he contemplated for a while his grave but genial visage, and smiled as his reflected face broadened or lengthened grotesquely and his pointed beard wagged in the waves of the water.

"This," said he at last, "shall be a place for pauses in city life. Here shall be a no-thoroughfare court, a lurking-place for shy respectability, for proud poverty; not quite for neediness, but for those who want and would, but will not."

Boston was laid out; the streets named themselves. This court chanced to be called Dulwich Court, which soon degraded itself to Dullish, and so it remained in nature and in name.

Whitegift Waddy, and Mehitabel, his wife, floating purposeless waifs through the new settlements, drifted into Dullish Court to live dull lives and then to meekly die. There was always one son in each generation of their family, an unwholesome lad, fed on remainder biscuits and stale mince pies. Still, it gradually became aristocratic to have come in with the Pilgrims. A certain consideration began to attach itself to the family, and the current Waddy, if such phrase may be used of so very stagnant a person, was always espoused by someone of a better class than his social condition could warrant. It was generally some pale schoolmistress, or invalided housekeeper of a great mansion, who became the better half of each gentle shopkeeper of Dullish Court.

These wives brought refinement and education with them; so that, at last, could they have sunk the shop, the Waddys would have been admitted as gentlefolk anywhere. They enjoyed, too, the consciousness of being better in rank than their neighbours. They never spoke of Whitegift as the cook, but as the Steward, or sometimes the Purveyor, of the *Mayflower*. They liked to walk through Beacon Street and smile placidly at the efforts of new people to win position by great houses, crowded balls and routs, and promotion marriages.

By-and-by it chanced that, quite contrary to rule, there were three sons in one generation playing in the puddles of Dullish Court and slyly filching dry gingerbread from the showcases of the old shop. It was a time when there was a flame in the land, and the elder twin of the three young Waddys, Whitegift by name, who had been early taken with tin soldiers and penny trumpets, awoke one morning after booziness to find himself, to his total surprise, with a red coat on his back and a king's shilling in his pocket. There was so little real martial ardour in his soul that he at once withered away, and being sent to the garrison of New York as a recruit of doubtful loyalty, he was there soon invalided. He finally dropped into the family trade and became a sutler. The Boston Waddys, saddened by his desertion of a cause they had vigour enough to support, soon forgot his existence—which does not at all imply that such existence terminated.

The other twin was apparently of the usual Waddy type; but when the great flame blazed forth at last unquenchable, he also took fire. He was a volunteer at Lexington and did active service, dropping several invaders in their bloody tracks. He was at once made sergeant in Captain Janeway's company, and gained the respect of his officers by his quick, ready energy. Ira was his name—Ira Waddy, the First.

Two months later, when the British were trying that uphill work at Bunker Hill for the third time, Captain Jane way and Sergeant Waddy waited rather too long. Three or four of the British rushed at Janeway with eyes staring for plunder. One of them stared at what he got and lay there staring, with his head down-hill. To bore this fellow had occupied Janeway's sword, and though Sergeant Waddy's clubbed musket could brain another assailant, it could not parry two bayonet thrusts. His breast could and did; so that Janeway felt nothing more than a scratch, when, with a murderous stamp of the left foot, another soldier ran the sergeant through. Just then a rush of flying Yankees came by and cleared the spot of foes. The captain had a moment to kneel by his preserver and hear him gasp some broken words:

"Mother! Take care of them, captain. Oh, Mary, Mary!"

When, after the surrender of Boston, Captain, now Colonel, Janeway called on that Mary with the news of her lover's death and his last words, she knew her life was widowed. There was nothing in the power of a man of wealth and growing distinction that the colonel did not offer her. She rejected all with a New England woman's quiet independence and mild self-reliance. To become a schoolmistress, as she did, was only to return to her original destiny.

Janeway remained her friend. He alone knew her secret. She was one of those strangely spiritual beings who interfere like dreamy visions in the inventive, busy business of Yankee life. She had a great, ennobling sorrow. Her lover had been a martyr of two religions. He had died for his country and for his friend. It may be said he died instinctively; but Mary knew that only the noble and the brave have noble and brave instincts.

To most people, Mary was only a pale schoolmistress. One person, however, met her on terms of devoted respect. Governor Janeway, the pre-eminently practical and successful man, found in her society what he found not with his gorgeous wife. She became the Cassandra of young Janeway—who went to the bad, it is true, but long after her death—and the kindly guide of his infant child.

Late in life she married Benajah Waddy, the youngest brother of the three. Janeway had made him bookkeeper, secretary, agent, but he had finally, after his mother's death, dwindled into the old shop. Mary, considering herself his brother's widow, came to a Hebraical, religious conclusion as to her duty. With entire simplicity of heart, she told Benajah that they ought to be married. As a matter of course, they were. The usual wife found, also, in process of time, their only son, Benajah, and married him. These both died, leaving their only son, Ira Waddy, to the charge of his aged and widowed grandmother, Mary, widow in heart of Ira the First.

Her grandson was named Ira after his great-uncle, the soldier. By-and-by it was discovered that a wide river in India bore the same name, and young Waddy was attracted toward his namesake. The old influence which, now reviving, made his blood hot as flame, urged him to know the land not merely of the citron and myrtle, but of spice and pungent condiments. His grandmother lavished upon him all the beautiful tenderness of her long-suppressed and desolated love, and then she died.

Ira Waddy's hot ardency of nature could not bear coolly any wrong. Wrong came to him. It would have extinguished an ancestor of the Whitegift class. Him it only kindled to counter-fire. He had his great quarrel with life, as many men have; he, in his young life. The Janeways had always been kind to him; so had their neighbours, the Beldens. In childish sports and youthful intercourse with the children of both families, he had often talked with enthusiasm of tropic splendours and India, his destined abode. When the world of his early associations became too narrow for him—too narrow because there his wrong would meet and hurtle him daily—then he thought again of India, and tropic indolence, and thoughtless people. Being an orphan and without kin, he could go where he chose. He chose India.

There, as the years passed, he became rich and powerful, a nabob, a merchant prince; but with all that this tale has no concern—it is written merely to chronicle the facts of his Return.

CHAPTER III
IN WHICH MR. WADDY REACHES HALIFAX AND MEETS WITH A MISADVENTURE

THE *Niagara* was running into Halifax.

It was early of a bright summer morning, and all the passengers came on deck, joyous with hopes of *terra firma*. There was our hero, Mr. Ira Waddy; there were two shipboard friends of his, Harry Dunston and Gilbert Paulding; there was the Budlong family, to wit: old De Flournoy Budlong; Mrs. De Flournoy Budlong, his second wife, luxuriantly handsome, and greatly his junior; Tim De Flournoy Budlong, and Arabella De Flournoy Budlong; and accompanying them was M. Auguste Henri Miromenil de Châteaunéant.

They all looked fresh and well-dressed in shore toggery. The Budlongs, particularly, were in full bloom. They were always now in full bloom, and meant the world should fully know they were returning from Europe with fashion and the fashions, with a gallery of pictures and a Parisian pronunciation. Old Budlong had once been a brisk young clerk, lively and lucky. He was called Flirney then. He had traded in most things and all had yielded him pelf. He was now a capitalist, fat and uneasy, with a natural jollity which he thought unbecoming his position and endeavoured to suppress. Budlong in full bloom was as formal as a ball bouquet.

It was under the régime of the second wife that the Budlongs had blossomed. After one season of gorgeous grandeur, but doubtful triumph, at home, they, or rather the master-she of their social life, determined to be stamped into undoubted currency by the cachet of Europe and Paris. They went, were *parisinés*, and were now returning, wiser and worse. They were now the De Flournoy B.'s, and brought with them De Châteaunéant, as attaché of mother and step-daughter, either or both. Old Bud, on marital and paternal grounds, disliked the Gaul.

Halifax is dull and provincial, but any land ho! is charming after a voyage. Old Budlong knew all about Mr. Waddy's wealth and position. He had lavished much of his style of civility, with much sincere good will, upon him on board ship and now was urgent that he should join the ladies and himself in their promenade ashore.

"Thank you," said Waddy, "but I have promised to take a tramp with your boy and these gentlemen," and he indicated Dunstan and Paulding.

So De Châteaunéant carried the day. Old Budlong walked in advance, inquiring the way, while his wife and daughter followed, making a cheerful glare of ankles through the muddy streets.

"Isn't it delightful to be ashore?" remarked Miss Arabella to Auguste Henri.

"Yese, mees. I am mose pleese to be out of ze ice-bugs. Ah, mademoiselle,"—as Arabella made a lofty lift over a puddle,—"vous avez le pied d'une sylphide."

Mr. Waddy and his companions soon exhausted the town. They lunched substantially on land fare, and having still time, went to drive, Dunstan and Paulding in one drag, Mr. Waddy and Tim in another. The first signal-gun recalled them. The two friends, whose steed was a comparative Bucephalus to the others' Rosinante, drew rapidly out of sight. The rear coachman was flogging his beast into a clumsy canter, when just as they passed a little jetty near some fishing-huts, they saw a child fall from the end into deep water.

"We can't let the child drown," said Mr. Waddy, stopping the coachman.

"He's none of ours. We must catch the ship. Perhaps he can swim," rejoined Timothy.

But it was evident he couldn't; there was no other help in sight. In an instant, Mr. Waddy was on the jetty, coat, waistcoat, and hat off; in another, he was fighting the tide for the drowning life.

Tim was no more selfish a fellow than is the rule with the sons of such merchants, and especially such step-mothers. He would, perhaps, have stayed by Mr. Waddy had that gentleman been in positive danger, but seeing that he was not only not drowning, but had the child safe by the hair, Tim whipped up and got on board just in time.

Cunarders do not wait for passengers who choose to go a-ducking after top-heavy children. Tim told his story. Mrs. Budlong and most of the commercial gentry rather laughed at Mr. Waddy. Dunstan and Paulding said nothing to them. They, however, seemed to have an opinion on the subject which prevented them from any further interchange of cigars with Master Timothy. Dunstan looked up Chin Chin, Mr. Waddy's Chinese servant, and by dint of pulling his ears and cue and saying Hi yah! a great many times, made him understand that his master was left, and he, Chin Chin, must pack up the traps, and for the present obey the cue-puller.

It was a very tender and beautiful thing to see how Mr. Waddy raised the insensible boy up from the boat below to the jetty. He wrapped the dripping object without scruple in his own very neat and knowing travelling jacket and carried him toward the mother, who had seen the accident from a distance and was running wildly toward them. She clasped the child to her breast, and, at the beating of her heart, life seemed suddenly to thrill through the saved one. He opened his eyes and smiled through his gasping agony.

Then the mother turned, seized Mr. Waddy in an all-round embrace, and gave him a stout fisherwoman's smack. It was a first-class salute for the returning hero.

He disentangled himself from this codfishy network; then, looking up, he suddenly fell to swearing violently in a variety of Oriental languages. The *Niagara* was just off under full headway. Two men, probably Dunstan and Paulding, were waving their handkerchiefs from the quarter-deck.

Mr. Waddy stopped swearing as suddenly as he had begun and burst into a roar of laughter; then he looked ruefully at his shirt.

The fisherwoman was occupied in punching the child's ribs and standing it on its head. It was spouting water like the fountain of Trevi, and gurgling out lusty screams that proved the efficacy of the treatment.

"Mrs. Hawkins," said Waddy, becoming conscious that he had observed her name over her door in his momentary *coup d'œil* before he sprang into the water; "Mrs. Hawkins, I am wet; you will have to dry me."

"Why, so you are," said the lady, "wet as a swab. Sammy, you jest git up an' go in the shop, an' don't you be fallin' overboard ag'in an' botherin' the gentleman."

She accompanied this advice with a box on the ear of the sobbing Sammy, which started Trevi again.

Without much ceremony or disappearance into a tiring-room, Mr. Waddy doffed his wet clothes and donned the toggery of the widow's eldest son. His cigar-case, well filled with cheroots, had fortunately escaped with his coat. He lighted his first, and sat waiting patiently while Mrs. Hawkins displayed his wet raiment before her cooking stove and turned the articles judiciously to toast on either side. Let us observe him as he sits.

He is rather young for a nabob. Many of the nabobs are lymphatic and wheezy, as well as old, and that without reference to the place of their nabobery, whether Canton, Threadneedle, or Wall Street. Mr. Waddy was none of these—he was alert, athletic, and thirty-seven. It is a grand thing to have had one's full experience and having chased all flying destinies through the bush, to have caught one and hold it safely in the hand, while the catcher is still young and strong enough to handle and tame the captive. Mr. Waddy looked strong and active enough to catch and tame anything. But some things are tamed only with delicacy and tenderness. Was he destitute of these? At this moment, there was no exhibition of any trait beyond nonchalant patience, such as men who have had to deal with Asiatics or Spanish Americans, necessarily acquire. As the last film of his smoke-puff exhales from his lips, they close under the yellow-brown moustache into an expression of firmness, and perhaps of pride. It was easy to see that firm might become stern, and pride might harshen bitterly, if treachery should betray generosity and repel candour.

Tossing his cheroot-end into the stove, he allows an interregnum for reverie. He leans his head upon his hand; his thick brown hair half hides the keen sparkle of his grey eyes; the lines of his mouth soften. He is thinking probably of welcomes from old friends, of pilgrimages to old shrines. Suddenly he throws down his hand; the proud expression closes again about his lips, his face hardens, hardens——

"Brown man, what makes you look so ugly and black?" says Sammy, loquitur. "Ma, I know he wants to kill me for wettin' his clothes," and Sammy wept boo! hoo!

"Don't cry, my boy," said Mr. Waddy, and putting his hand into a pocket he thought his own, he drew out not the expected purse containing the presentable shilling, but a strip of pigtail tobacco. "Am I brown? I am the Ancient Mariner. I have been where the sun bakes men as brown as that loaf of gingerbread. Here are two shillings out of my vest pocket. Keep one yourself and buy that loaf from your mother with the other. My mother used to bake gingerbread and my father sold it, years ago, when I was white, not ginger-coloured."

So Ira and Sammy came to terms of peace and good will and munched together.

"I kind er guess your things is dry now, capting," said Mrs. Hawkins. "I'll jest put the flatiron to that air shirt and make it as slick as a slide. Salt water don't take sterch or them collars would stan' right up."

While Mr. Waddy was recovering his habiliments, Isaiah Hawkins, the widow's eldest son, came in. He owned a small coaster and was to sail that afternoon for Portland. He came to get his traps.

"Can you take a passenger?" inquired Mr. Waddy, after the usual preliminary greetings.

"Wal, capting," replied Hawkins, with much deliberation, "I dunno as I could, an' I dunno as I couldn't. What kind a feller is this ere passenger? Kin he eat pork an' fish?"

"I'm the man," explained Mr. Waddy. "I should think I could eat pork and fish. I've lived in Boston."

"Wal, capting, come along if yer like," said Hawkins heartily, "an' it shan't cost yer a durned cent. 'Tain't every feller I'd take, but I feel kinder 'bleeged to yer fer pickin' up Sam."

Mr. Waddy would not consent to be a dead-head, but took pay passage at once, to start at two. Meanwhile he strolled about the town, and climbing the steep glacis, admired the glorious bay and the impregnable fort. He was entering when his way was stopped by the sentinel.

"No one admitted without special order," announced that functionary.

"My old friend Mr. Waddy has special entrée everywhere!" cried a passing officer, laying his hand on Ira's shoulder. "My dear fellow, you wouldn't let me thank you at Inkerman for dropping that Cossack. Now I intend to pepper you with gratitude."

"Oh, no! we never mention it, Granby," retorted Ira, warmly grasping the extended hand, "unless you need reminding how you dropped the rhinoceros who wouldn't drop me. By the way, I've had a match-box made of his horn."

He pulled out his cigar-case and the match-box. They each took a cigar and walked off together to Major Granby's quarters, as coolly as if the reciprocal life-saving they had recalled was an everyday business.

"How in the name of Mercury came you here?" asked the major, after they were seated.

"Ginger beer—gingerbread, beer," murmured Waddy abstractedly. "Bass' Pale Ale. Yes—ah, well!"

"What, ho! Patrick!" called the major. "Here's Mr. Waddy come back and wants his ale!"

While Patrick grinned a cheerful recognition and drew the cork, Mr. Waddy explained his position and the gingerbread allusion.

"I sail at two for Portland in the *Billy Blue Nose*," he concluded. "Why won't you come and see me in the States?"

"Why not? I'll join you when you please," assented Granby instantly. "I already have a furlough. I wish I could start to-day."

"Come by the next steamer, to-day fortnight," suggested Ira, "and meet me in Boston at the Tremont House. I'm really as much a stranger as you; but they all know me. We'll see the lions together."

"You'll have to be a ladies' man, for my sake," said the major. "I've heard the American women are the loveliest of the world, and I've determined to see for myself. I thought, before I saw you, of dropping in at Newport this summer. That's the mart, I hear."

"Certainly, we'll go there and everywhere," agreed Ira. "What do you say to a partnership for matrimonial speculation? You put in good looks, good name, and glory. I contribute money—the prize, of course, to be mine."

"You say nothing about wit," the major pointed out. "Modest! As to good looks, these are perhaps degenerate days, but you'll do very well for an Antinous with whiskers, and I used constantly in Rome to be mistaken for the Apollo, in costume of the period."

"Well, Apollo, I leave you to study attitudes," said Waddy, rising. "I must be off. Good-bye! To-day three weeks."

"So long! Here, Pat! pack up a carpet-bag for Mr. Waddy and put in some of those short shirts. My six-feet-one beats you by three inches."

The *Billy Blue Nose* was quite ready. Mr. Waddy was also ready and just stepping into the boat when he heard Sammy's voice:

"Say, mister! gimme another shilling to buy gingerbread!"

We leave the reader to judge whether the prayer went unanswered.

CHAPTER IV
A GENTLE LADY OF FORTUNE DECIDES TO FACE A STORM

THE afternoon was hot and sulky. Still, as the party had fixed that day for leaving The Island, they would not change their plan. Old Dempster said there would certainly be "considerable of a blow."

All the party had longed for a storm; the young ladies had rhapsodised about billows and breakers and driving spray and heroic encounters with warring elements. Now that the long roll of premonitory surges was crashing in sullenly on Black Rock Head and Wrecker's Point, they seemed to shrink a little from billows unsunlit. Grandeur was too much for them. To recline on the rocks under a parasol held by a gentle cavalier, this was gay and dressy and afforded the recumbent and her attendant knight indefinite possibilities. But ladies are not lovely in submarine armour, and muslins limply collapse when salt showers come whirling in from shattered waves. The great wild terror of the certain storm made itself felt among the gay party. They were quite willing to hasten their departure and pass the night quietly at Loggerly. They would spend also a quiet next day there and take the train on the second morning for Portland and Boston.

Miss Sullivan preferred to stay for the promised entertainment. She seemed already a little excited out of her usual tranquil reserve by the thought that Nature was to act a wild drama for her benefit. Besides, apart from the storm, she was willing to pass one solitary day on the rocks and along the beach. She also longed for one last master-view from the mountain above Dempster's house. She was glad to see all these without the intrusion of gaiety. It may have been a mood; it may have been character. She would visit, for perpetual recollection, the best spots undisturbed; a storm would be clear gain. Mr. Dempster promised to drive her over to Loggerly next evening, rain or shine.

Au revoir! and they were off, some walking, some already mounted into the great farm wagon. They had a very lively time through the delicate birch woods. Miss Julia Wilkes was quite sure she had seen a deer. Blooming lips were brighter for the strawberries they crushed; rosy fingers rosier for plucking the same. When they reached the open country and were all seated in the wagon, taking the down-hills at a gallop, and the up-hills at an impetus, Julia turned to her mother, that excellent, gossipy person.

"Miss Sullivan has a strange fancy," said she, "to wander about alone in wild places. Did you notice how almost handsome she was to-day?"

"Yes," put in the *fortis Gyas* Cutus; "she looked like a cheerful Banshee, inspired at the thought of a storm."

"Mary Sullivan was nobly handsome once," said Mrs. Wilkes, "and will be soon again, I hope, now that she is rich and done with all family troubles."

"Is she very rich?" asked Cloanthus Fortisque, friend of Gyas. "I'm sorry I'm so much afraid of her. She may be sweet as ice-cream, but she is colder. A feller couldn't sail in with much chance."

Miss Julia pouted a little at this ingenuous remark of Fortisque and devoted herself to Gyas Cutus for the rest of the journey.

———————

It was lonely at Dempster's when the gay party was gone. The house looked singularly small and mean. Mrs. Dempster was baking wondrous bread; bread for which all the visitors had gone away bulkier. Miss Miranda Dempster was up to her elbows in strawberries. She was a magnificent lioness of a woman, with a tawny mane of redundant locks.

The kitchen was close and the hot, heavy atmosphere affected Miss Sullivan's views as to the quality of her hostess's bread. She walked out upon the little meadow, a bit of tender culture between the forest and the rude and rocky shore. Old Dempster and Daniel, his son, were hurrying their hay into the ox-cart. The oxen seemed to stand unnecessarily knockkneed and feeble in the blasting heat. Yet the sun was obscured and there came puffs of breeze from seaward. But these were puffs explosive, sultry, volcanic, depressing.

As Miss Sullivan approached, Dempster was tossing up an enormous mass of hay to Daniel. A puff of wind caught it and one half "diffused to empty air," making air no longer empty but misty with hay-seed, and aromatic with mild fragrance. Dempster shook himself and stood leaning on his pitchfork. He was a grand old yeoman, worthy to be the father of heroes. The Island, though not a solitary one, had been to him a Juan Fernandez. He was a contriver of all contrivances, a builder of all that may be built. He farmed, he milled, he fished, he navigated in shapely vessels of his own shaping; his roof-tree was a tree of his own woods, felled and cleft by himself. He had split his own shingles as easily as other men mend a toothpick; with these he had tented his roof-tree over. Miss Sullivan and he were great friends, and now, as she drew near, he looked at her with kindly eyes.

"See, Miss Sullivan," said he, "them oxen has stopped chewin' the cud—another sure sign of a storm. The wind is sou'west. It'll be short, but hot an' heavy—a kind er horriken."

"If the storm is severe, what will all these fishing-vessels do?" she asked. "I have counted nearly a hundred this afternoon."

"Most on 'em will go birds'-nestin' 'round in the bays an' coves along shore. Some on 'em alluz gits caught, an' that's what makes me feel kind er anxious now. You see, my boy Willum has been buyin' a schooner up to New Brunswick, with a pardner of his, and he's jest as like as not to be takin' her down to Boston about now."

"I hope not!" cried Miss Sullivan, shuddering involuntarily in the hot chill of another isolated blast.

"Wal, worryin' won't mend nothin'," said the father, with stoic calmness. "Come, Dan'l, we must hurry up with this 'ere hay," and the two fell to work again; but the face of the elder man was very grave as he glanced, from time to time, at the grey sky and sullen sea.

Miss Sullivan strolled on across the meadow to Black Rock Head. There she had often sat in brilliant days and sent her looks and thoughts a-dreaming beyond the misty edge of the ocean world. To-day a strange, dismal heaviness in the air made dreams nightmares. Perpetual calm seemed destined to dwell upon the ocean, so unruffled was its surface and unsuggestive of storms to be. Looking down from the Head, Miss Sullivan would scarcely have discerned the great, slow surges, lifting and falling monotonously. They made themselves felt, however, when they met the opponent crag. A vast chasm stood open in its purple rocks, and as the lazy waves fell upon the unyielding shore, they flowed in, filling this cavernous gulf almost to the brim with foaming masses. Then, as the surge deliberately withdrew, these ambitious waters, abandoned and unsupported, plunged downward in a wild whirlpooling panic, stream overwhelming stream, all seething together furiously, hissing, roaring, thundering, until again they met the incoming breaker, and again essayed as vainly to rise above control and overcome the enduring land.

Mists, slowly uprising, had given sunset a dull reception, and the great southeastern cloud-bank was growing fast heavier and heavier. Puffs of driving fog began to hide the mountain and lower down upon the Dempster house. Darkness fell, and at last Miss Sullivan was driven in.

CHAPTER V
A WRECK AND A RESCUE

ALL night the storm did its tyrannous work over sea and land; all night, around old Dempster's house, it howled its direful menaces. But the house stood firm, for it had been built to withstand the shock of any storm; only shivered now and then as the gale smote it with heavier hand, then tore on its way lamenting.

More than once Miss Sullivan awoke and lay listening to the storm's wild voices—voices which recalled the past—voices whispering, pleading, sighing, moaning to be heard again and again answered. And they were answered—answered with bitter moans and tears, and at last with prayers for patience and peace, and, if need were, for pardon.

Neither Mrs. Dempster nor Miranda understood the enthusiasm of Miss Sullivan for storms and breakers. There were several things they would rather do than venture out next morning: the chief of which was to stay at home.

Old Dempster looked uneasily at the cloud-drift. The wind was as furious as ever, but the rain came only in keen showers.

"These 'ere sou'-easters," said he, "never last long at this time o' the year. It'll be clear as moonshine by long about noon. But ef you've got your mind set on goin' out, I'll rig you out so you'll be dry as a rooster. Dan'l, go down to the mill an' bring up them short overhauls."

Dan'l brought up a great coat of yellow, oiled canvas, and a tarpaulin with a flap like the tail of a Barbary sheep. Mrs. Dempster supplied a pair of Dan'l's fishing boots, outgrown by him in one bare-footed summer, but still impervious.

Miss Sullivan, a person very critical in her toilet, hesitated a little at this unaccustomed attire. However, it was the sensible style. Miranda aided her in encasing herself. Stiffish were both overhauls and boots; stiffness itself, at the first interview.

When they returned to the kitchen to stand inspection, a sound was heard as if the kettle of dried apples boiling on the stove had suddenly bubbled and sputtered over. It was Dan'l, utterly unable to control his laughter. He immediately disappeared, and was heard in the wood-shed endeavouring to whistle, but constantly breaking down into a snicker.

"Poor Dan'l!" said Miss Sullivan; "I must look very droll, indeed."

"Wal," said Mrs. Dempster, "you are kind er like my idee of a Mormon—I mean one o' them folks in the pictures with gals' heads an' more like a codfish to the other end. Now if one o' them gals should make herself decent with a set of overhauls—an' massy knows she wants suthin' to cover her—she'd look jest as pooty as you do. Wouldn't she, old man?"

To avoid other comparisons as complimentary to mermen or maids, Miss Sullivan ran from her circle of amused admirers and, passing among the pathless cucumber vines of the little garden, began awkwardly to climb the fence that kept any amphibious rodent monster of the deep from predatory excursions among the radishes and hollyhocks. Beyond the garden, a thicket of wild fruit vines nearly closed the shoreward path. Drops of rain hung heavy, crushing the bushes with pearly wreaths. A few raspberries were only waiting one sunny day to take their dull purple crimson of ripeness. It was wet work to penetrate by the obliterated path. Miss Sullivan, however, crowded steadily forward.

When the rustling of her passage through the thicket ceased, she could hear the neighbour crashing of breakers. Black Rock Head rose to the north of the rocky cove, home of Dempster's boat. Southward stood other headlands, and southern-most, Wrecker's Point, where all the fury of surges driven by the southeast gale would be felt. When the mingled mist, spray, and rain were drifted away for a moment, and shrank to give space to a great, howling blast, she could see a lofty white ghostly object, like a ship in full sail, dimly visible, suddenly lift itself against the dark front of the Head. Then it sank away, dashed to nothingness of foamy wreck. A hollow roar came, as the cavernous cleft of the Head was overcrowded with the breaker, and, gushing up, the mass of uprising waters overwhelmed the promontory and, spreading, mantled over its smooth surfaces and tore in many cataracts down its chasms to the sea. The Head, through veils of mist, seemed like a distant dome mountain of snow.

Black Rock Head was evidently unapproachable, so Miss Sullivan faced the blast and its blinding, driving spray, for a sheltered spot farther on toward Wrecker's Point. She found that her foreground of vision of storm-experiences was crowding itself with quite unsatisfactory detail. There was no sieve of trees by the shore to filter the salt showers. Sometimes there was but a narrow path between slippery slopes of grass and rounded rocks glistening with the touch of the more ambitious breakers. As she passed by these perilous places, an unlooked-for wash of water would come hungrily up and hasten hungrily back, willing to sweep away fragile womanhood. The morning was well advanced when, with slow and difficult progress, the lady who, after her bold vigour of devotion to her object, merits, at least for the nonce, the title of our heroine, reached Wrecker's Point.

Of seeing much that storms may do she had had her heart's desire. All the dread fury of maddened winds had burst upon her till she had tottered back to some shelter of intervening rock, appalled at tempest terrors that houselings never know. In tremulous pauses, when the gale was still, she had heard the coming thunder of the long breaker, coming awfully because an infinite ocean drove it on; and as this went bursting like an upward avalanche from crag to crag beyond, in the silence while the next billow was lifting she had heard those dreadful ocean voices surrounding her, a wild atmosphere of remorse—of remorse unpardoned and forever unpardonable for all the murderous wrongs of ocean to the world. And after these came the bewildering whirl of spray and rain, the crash, the hissing fall, and then the great blow of the breaker like a knell. It hammered at the world's foundations, until that solid world seemed an unstable thing to tread.

The rain had ceased when Miss Sullivan reached the Point. It was clearing, and she could look more widely over the immense agitation and sway of the lurid sea. She sat for an hour or wandered about over perils of wave-worn crags, that waves were now striving vainly to shatter. At last she remembered that she had the beach still to visit before her return. Her path thither was through a wood, tangled and bewildering with vines and underbrush. The storm was now almost a calm, but the thunder of the surges followed her as she hastened along the dripping trail. Penetrating slowly through the wood by paths of uneasy footing, she began to distinguish the distant part of the beach. It formed one end of a parallelogram, whose sides were dark ranges of low, broken precipice and the farther end the blank of sea. Opposite her, the precipice continued up into a wooded mountain. The sun was just breaking forth and scattering a slender, illumined scarf of mist, that wavered in among the trees of the mountain-side, and melted into that ever-fresh wonder of beauty, the calm sky of summer.

There was much rubbish strewn along the beach. Miss Sullivan could see old waterlogged slabs, logs purple with long drowning, pieces of spar, a plank or so. As she descended and looked over the nearer sands, she saw more rubbish; more than usual, perhaps of a recent wreck. Such a storm could hardly pass without touching the pockets of jolly underwriters—less jolly over their noon sandwich as the telegraph told of ships ashore.

The path began to skirt the edge of the broken cliff, and finally descended rapidly, by a series of dangerous stepping places, toward the level. It was quite evident there had been a wreck. The water deepened very slowly out from the shore, and each swell, as it swept in, drove along bits or masses of wreckage, and retiring, dragged them back, to be again heaved farther up.

Miss Sullivan had never before seen a wreck. She suddenly seemed very curious to examine this one nearer,—passionately curious, indeed,—and began to leap down the hillside rather precipitately. However, she was now used to Dan'l's boots; otherwise her headlong speed would have been dangerous. She found it rather deep trudging in the sand, deeper and more difficult as she ran rapidly down after the returning waves; and she found it a struggle for her own life in the undertow, as she resolutely plunged forward and, grasping some wrecked fragments, fought with so much desperate womanish force as she had to drag them in to shore and safety.

These fragments had lashed to them the body of a man.

The sea had done with this object what it chose; it was weary of its plaything, and now aided her in her merciful task. For many moments she was ready to despair and drown; but hope was her ally, and a nervous, unsuspected strength, and at last she gained a firm footing and dragged the man away from the waves up on the wet sand.

She sank exhausted in a dizzy trance, blinded and fainting. It had been a terrible, heart-rending agony of combat—a very doubtful strife for two lives with the hungry sea.

Starting up at last, she seemed to shrink from quieter examination of the wrecked person. But conquering fear or superstition in a moment's struggle, she knelt beside him. His arm was raised, covering his face, and his clenched hand held something that was attached by a strand of silk around his neck. As she removed the arm, the hand relaxed in hers and a small book fell from it; she pulled it from the silk and laid it hastily by.

Parting the hair from the sadly bruised and battered face, she looked vainly into closed eyes for any light of life. She laid her hand where the heart should be beating; she placed her lips close, nay, almost touching, livid lips, to catch a faintest breath; she did all those passionately desperate things that one may do, feeling that another life may depend on each lapsing moment's effort. She had nothing to cut the lashings which bound him to the wreck, and tore at them furiously, vainly, with her teeth. There was a hard, dry sobbing in her throat, and her features worked convulsively as she paused, exhausted, and gazed down at that white, quiet face. She was ready again to despair. She could not leave him; would no help come? The sun seemed oppressively hot and cruel—a staring, insulting fullness of daylight.

Help was coming. She heard a cheerful woman's voice singing a negro melody in the wood. Miranda had evidently expected that Miss Sullivan's circuit would bring her to the beach and had come to join her.

Miss Sullivan essayed to scream, but could not. Miranda came to the bank, and seeing her standing like a ghost, vainly striving to beckon, divined the whole in an instant and sprang down the steps.

"Is he dead?" cried Miranda.

The formalising of a dreaded thought into words makes its terrors doubly terrible.

"Dead! I fear so," said Miss Sullivan, very slowly and with a shiver.

"He shan't die if we can help it," said Miranda resolutely. "Here, Miss Mary, you run right up to the second field. Up there, Uncle Jake's out with the boys, seeing if they can mow after the shower. Bring 'em down quick—I'll cut him loose."

Suiting act to word, she whipped out a jagged penknife of schoolmarm days from her pocket, and began to saw at the lashings.

Miss Sullivan clambered, panting, up the cliff and plunged into the wood. Presently she appeared at a run, followed by Uncle Jake and the two boys—biggish boys of six feet two.

Miranda had cut the lashings of rotten stuff. Uncle Jake supported the man in his arms. He was perfectly insensible.

"He's not dead," said Uncle Jake.

"He'll live; I know he'll live!" cried Miranda.

"Hooray!" shouted the two boys tumultuously—a view-halloo for a found life.

"Thank God!" said Miss Sullivan, with a quick, irrepressible sob of thankfulness.

CHAPTER VI
IN WHICH MISS SULLIVAN FINDS MANY REASONS
FOR DEPARTURE

UNCLE JAKE and his giant progeny made light of their burden, all the half-mile to old Dempster's. They were confident, feeling their own vigorous blood beating healthily from end to end of their great bodies, that no man, not dead, could die. In their experience as farmers and fishermen, they had seen much more dangerous hurts recovered from than any of the stranger's.

"He's pretty well bunged up an' has swallered an almighty lot o' salt water; but that'll do him good an' cure the bruises. Why, I shouldn't wonder," continued Uncle Jake, gradually talking himself into positiveness, "ef he was jumpin' 'round by day after to-morrer, as spry as a two-year-old. He ain't a sailor. I kind er guess he was a passenger aboard some 'long-shore craft. That wrecked stuff looked like it belonged to some Down East schooner. I hope it warn't Bill Dempster's. Now, Mirandy, you take good keer o' this here chap an' p'r'aps he'll be a-buckin' up to yer, when he's so's to be 'round."

Miranda and Miss Sullivan smiled. Uncle Jake was evidently a little more concerned than he pretended, and chatted to keep up their spirits. Once or twice when the bearers paused to shift hands or rest a moment, their burden seemed to make a futile attempt toward life. There was a tremor of eyelid and lip—perhaps a slight unclosing of the eye. Still, if there was any change, deathliness soon came again.

Miss Sullivan and Miranda ran on to make preparations.

"I think," said the latter, "that we'd better put him in your room, if you still mean to go, as you decided yesterday."

"I must go," replied the other, with a quick intaking of the breath, "unless I can be of some service to this gentleman." Was it her fine instinct that had recognised the gentleman?

"I don't see what you can do more than mother and I will—except that you have kinder, pleasanter ways," Miranda assured her. "P'r'aps this man will turn out to be a sailor 'long shore, after all, and we'll know how to nuss him better than you would."

"Well," said Miss Sullivan, "we shall see;" but it was evident that in her heart she was quite certain he was no sailor.

Mrs. Dempster flurried about and had everything ready in the invalid's room by the time Uncle Jake arrived. The three men carried their burden into his hospital, while the women waited anxiously for a report. Life or Death?

Old Dempster and Dan'l at this moment returned from catching and feeding White Socks and preparing the buggy for Miss Sullivan's journey. While they were hearing the history of the rescue, Uncle Jake came out with a cheerful look.

"He ain't no sailor," he announced. "Here's his pocket-book with three hundred an' fifty dollars in gold. You just take that, old woman, and don't let Dan'l use any on 'em for buttons to his new swaller-tail. Wal, Miss Sullivan, I guess your man'll git well. He's breathin' reg'lar, but don't seem to know nothin' yit."

Miranda went to take her place as nurse by the bedside. By-and-by, her mother needing her for a few moments, she called Miss Sullivan.

The wrecked man was beginning to stir about uneasily. He murmured and muttered names, evidently those uppermost in his waking thought. Life was struggling to regain voluntary control. He was feverish. Miss Sullivan gave him from time to time spoonfuls of stimulant; his weakness and exhaustion needed this. It was a new position for her, and she managed rather awkwardly,—more awkwardly than one would have expected who knew her usual deftness. Once, when his eyes again half opened, she shrank away, and when he again became delirious and rejected his restorative and went on speaking wildly and incoherently, mingling names, words of hate and words of love and words of dreary despair, she burst into a sudden passion of excited tears and called Miranda to come immediately and relieve her. She evidently was not fit to be a calm nurse to the stranger: a fact sufficiently curious, since her temperament was quite the nursely one. But perhaps she was too much concerned for her protégé.

The afternoon hastened away. The sufferer seemed momentarily improving. He had now fallen into a quiet sleep. Mr. Dempster appeared to ask the plans of his guest—to go or not to go?

Miss Sullivan said she felt that she could be of no real service; she was, of course, much interested in the final recovery of her waif, but she could have news of him from Miranda; she ought not to detain her friends at Loggerly.

What she did not say, in spite of a somewhat evident anxiety to find reasons for departure, was that she did not dare trust herself to encounter the stranger on his recovery, so shaken was she by certain inward tremors, so prostrated in strength and spirits—the result, no doubt, of her efforts in his behalf. An instinct of self-protection urged to flight. She gave the word, "Go."

White Socks and the buggy came to the door. Dan'l stepped forward with a bunch of hollyhocks, pink, yellow, and purple. He got a very unexpected kiss—unexpected by giver and receiver.

"Thank you for your boots, Dan'l. I could not have gone a step without them."

There was a very blushing Dan'l, a very pensive Dan'l, a very manly Dan'l, a very like-a-first-lover Dan'l, about the premises that evening. He doubled his fists and said "Durn it!" very often, but always ended with a pleased smile. Dan'l was having his first glimpses into fairyland; his world seemed enchanted, as he wandered out through the ferns to sunset—strawberries his pretence.

Everyone was sorry to part with Miss Sullivan. With Miranda especially, her adieux were most affectionate. These two had been engaged in the romantic duty of saving a life.

"Write me every day, Miranda," were Miss Sullivan's last words, and she quite blushed as she uttered them. "Write me every day and tell me how he does."

Old Dempster drove her away in the delicious summer evening. White Socks made good play and brought them into Loggerly at late twilight.

All the party greeted Miss Sullivan cordially and gaily asked her experiences of storm life. She did not dwell upon her share in the rescue—some occult influence seemed to hold her back from speaking of it—and soon retired. Extreme fatigue saved her from the excitement of dreams, and she sank into the blessedness of a sleep undisturbed by storminess either from within or without. Sleep and change of scene will draw a blank between her and the adventures of to-day: but she will hardly forget them. Mad storms by the maddened sea are not daily events in the lives of quiet ladies of fortune; nor does it happen to every promenader by a beach to be the point of safety whither a returning wanderer may drift away from his death.

After Miss Sullivan's disappearance, her companions all talked of her, as people always do of the dear departed.

"Odd idea, that of hers—to go out in the wet," observed Gyas. "How would you and I look, old Clo, taking a picturesque ducking?"

"Did anyone ever see you doing anything picturesque, Mr. Cutus?" inquired Miss Julia innocently.

"Pictures are done of him—lots of 'em by Scalper," said Cloanthus. "Scalper says his name describes him exactly—he's the best guy he can find. There—I wouldn't have told that, Gyas, if you hadn't called me old Clo. You know I don't like nicknames."

"I wonder Miss Sullivan never married," remarked someone, to end this controversy.

"Miss Sullivan has not been rich very long," said Mrs. Wilkes, in a tone to indicate that no further explanation was needed; "only since the death of her step-father. He had some property in Chicago which suddenly became of enormous value. He left everything to her. You know her own family were great people once, but lost caste and wealth by a transaction of her father's. After that, she was obliged to teach in a public school for a while. Then she became governess to Clara Waddie and Diana, Mr. Waddie's ward. When they went to Europe, she came to us."

"Yes!" said Julia, with ardency. "I was an immense little fool, till then. But, mamma, wasn't there a story of a love affair of hers, while she was young?"

"Horace Belden hinted something of the kind," replied her mother, "and that he was the object. But he is very willing to claim conquests. As soon as the news of her great inheritance came, while she was with us in Paris, Mr. Belden called upon her. He pretended great surprise that she was our governess and regret that he had not seen his old friend before."

"He knew it, I'm sure he did!" cried Julia. "Miss Sullivan and I met him twice in the Louvre, and both times he dodged—palpably. I could not understand why."

"Well," continued Mrs. Wilkes, serenely picking up her story where she had been interrupted, "with the news of the fortune came Mr. Belden. Miss Sullivan was in the salon with me. He went up to her with that soft manner which he thinks so irresistible. 'My dear Miss Mary,' he said, 'I had no idea that you were here with my friends. Permit me to be among the first to congratulate you. It seems that the Fates do not always err in distributing their good gifts. How long it is since we have met! Where have you been this age?' Mary received him rather icily; and afterwards she would never speak of him, except to say that they were neighbours in childhood. I suspect that it was merely his slights during her poverty that displeased her—I don't believe she was ever in love with him."

"Was not that the time when he was so attentive to Diana?" asked Julia.

"Yes, my dear," babbled the good, gossipy Mrs. Wilkes, "and she liked him, as débutantes are very apt to like men of the world; but Clara Waddie and Diana and Miss Sullivan were always together, and whenever Mr. Belden went, he found his 'old friend' cool and distant as possible. I don't think Mary ever spoke of him to Diana, but there came a sudden end of sentimental tête-à-têtes such as they had had in Switzerland, and when he proposed to Diana to go off and look at some picture, or point of view, she always made it a condition to invite Miss Sullivan."

"Ah, these duennas!" said the brave Gyas, who had frequently found his bravery of heart and toilet to become naught in their presence. "But who is this Diana? Is her other name Moonshine? I know everybody and don't know her. Where did you pick her up?"

"Pick her up!" exclaimed Julia, in wrath. "Diana! Why, she would hardly touch anyone with her parasol, except for friendship's sake—and she's the dearest girl! You'll see her this summer, but she won't let you talk to her, because you are not agreeable enough," and Miss Julia blushed a little the next moment and was sorry for her wrath at the brave Gyas.

"Is she rich?" asked the prudent Cloanthus.

"Of course; she is very rich. She owns Texas," replied Julia confidently.

"Texas!" echoed Cloanthus, bewildered by the spacious thought. "Isn't that a state or a country, or a part of Mexico, or something?"

"Perhaps it is," admitted Julia; "perhaps she only owns half of it. But I am sure I've heard her speak of riding for a day over her own land."

Mrs. Wilkes was now asleep in her chair—hence, and hence only, her silence. She awoke suddenly and reminded her friends of their early morning start. They separated for the night.

Next day, when the conductor of the railroad train came to Miss Sullivan for her fare, she transferred her purse from her bag to the pocket of her travelling dress. As she did so, she felt an unfamiliar object. It proved to be the book she had taken from the drowning man's hand, and, without thinking, dropped into her pocket. It had been protected by a covering of oiled silk. The stitches in drying had given way and the book was slipping out. She thought there could be no harm in her opening it.

It was an old, well-worn Testament. On the title-page was the inscription "M. Janeway to I. Waddy." It was very touching to think of this drowning man clinging to the last to this emblem of his religion, and perhaps token of an early love. No doubt it was in sympathy with some such thought as this that Miss Sullivan's hands began suddenly to tremble, and her eyes to fill with tears as she turned over the sacred pages.

The book opened naturally in her hand at a familiar passage; she read a few lines; then the hot tears blinded her and she put the book hastily away.

CHAPTER VII
A PEPPERY INVALID WHO DREAMS DREAMS AND BRINGS BAD NEWS

IN the morning Mr. Waddy awaked, and, looking feebly around, discovered Mrs. Dempster.

"Where is the other?" he asked, half rising and falling back disappointed.

Mrs. Dempster called her daughter.

Miranda came, splendidly fresh from her morning's duties in full air, and her tawny locks shaken about in dishevelled luxuriance.

"Not you," said Mr. Waddy, shrinking a little from her lioness aspect. "I want the other. She had a tarpaulin and yellow canvas clothes the first time, and then I saw her again here—I am sure it was here. Here! Where am I?"

He stopped and looked about him wildly.

"Why, you're in my house," responded Mrs. Dempster soothingly, "an' I hope you'll make yerself to hum. You've been drownded an' that was Miss Sullivan that found you. Ef she hadn't been kind er cur'us about goin' out to see how a storm feels, massy knows where you'd be now."

"Miss Sullivan?" repeated Mr. Waddy. "There is no one of that name who would take any trouble for me."

"She did take a sight er trouble, though," said the old lady, "an' some folks'd be more thankful for 't than you seem to be. 'Tain't every city lady that'll go wadin' 'round an' resk drownin' herself to haul out a man. Some of them other gals would 'a' sat down an' screamed."

"Madam," said Mr. Waddy, with weak testiness, "I am not acquainted with Miss Sullivan and did not ask her to save me."

"Wal, now!" said Mrs. Dempster to herself. "Sakes alive! What an ongrateful critter! I can't stan' it; but I s'pose he's sick and onreasonible."

So saying she marched out, and clattering pans soon banged a warlike accompaniment to her murmured wrath.

Miranda remained, and Mr. Waddy turned to her in a despairing search for information.

"You are sure that person in the tarpaulin was Miss Sullivan?" he questioned. "Sullivan, I think you said?"

Miranda nodded.

"Quite certain," she assured him.

"Then," murmured Waddy, "I've seen a ghost. I'm insane. I always wished to know what the feeling was. Now I have it. Bring a strait-jacket, quick! I'm dangerous! Hold me!"

And he sank back, looking excessively feeble and quite manageable.

Presently he seemed to revive a little.

"Miss Miranda," he continued, "how do you suppose I know your name?"

"Perhaps you heard mother call me," she suggested.

"No," said he, "I heard it in a dream, an exquisite dream, such as may come to us insane men to compensate us for losing our wakeful wits. My dream was this: I thought that I was lying powerless in the dominion of a wonderful delight—a delight not strange, but seemingly familiar as a fulfilled prophecy, whose fulfilment had been forever a lingering certainty. I was lying, trammelled by a willing motionlessness, in the loveliest glade of a wood fresh as Paradise. And then my trance, so content with its own happiness, was visited with happiness inexpressibly greater. It seemed that a face, well known, as to dreams of infancy a mother's sweet watchfulness may be,—that such a face, perhaps my own life-long dream of pureness personified, bent over me and seemed searching through my closed eyes, into my very soul, for the imperishable legends of my better life, written there beneath my earliest and holiest vows. I heard a voice, such as I may have dreamed the voice of an angel, and it said, 'Beautiful world of God! Why are we not happy?' Then all the vision faded into dimness and someone like you, you in fact, came between me and the angel, and the voice called you by your name, 'Miranda.'"

"It is a very pretty dream," said Miranda, as he stopped, visibly exhausted, "and truer than most dreams. When we were bringing you up from the beach, we rested several times in the wood, and Miss Sullivan, who seems to me like an angel, stooped over you to see whether you were reviving at all. I remember, too, that she said something like what you heard."

"Miss Sullivan," repeated Mr. Waddy, rather crossly; "a very respectable young woman, I've no doubt. But I don't know her—well, I must have been in a trance and seen old visions."

He remained silent for some time, buried in thought—not pleasant thought, to judge by his countenance.

"Princess Miranda," he resumed, at last, "what may be the name of your realm? Where am I? Is Duke Prospero without?"

"You're in father's house on The Island in Maine," answered Miranda simply. "There's father, now, just come back from taking Miss Sullivan to Loggerly."

"So she's gone without stopping to see whether I lived or died!" muttered Mr. Waddy. "I'm glad of it. Infernal bore! to have to thank her and pay compliments to some namby-pamby plough-girl. Let's see what I can give her—a six-inch cameo—a copy of Tennyson's poems—an annuity of ten bushels of tracts? She won't like money—I know these Yankee girls. This Miranda is another style. By curry!" asseverated he rapturously, "she is as grand as a lioness. Singularly like Hawkins's partner in the schooner. Ah, those poor fellows! Not one of them left, I'm afraid."

His reverie was interrupted by the entry of old Dempster, accompanied by his wife and Dan'l.

"Wal, sir," began the former, with brisk heartiness, "I'm glad to see you doin' better. Here's some money we found in your belt—three hundred an' fifty dollars. Count it, if you please."

"Never mind the money," said Waddy. "I would give that and much more to have news of the vessel I was wrecked in. Have you heard anything about her? She was a Down East schooner named the *Billy Blue Nose*."

"What might the name of her owner be?" asked Mr. Dempster. "One of my boys has been buyin' a schooner up to Halifax."

"Hawkins was the name; but he had a partner, a very fine young fellow, who told me he lived on this coast. He lashed me to the spar and stayed by me till she struck. His name was Dempster—William Dempster."

"Mother," said the old man, very solemnly, after a moment, "it's our boy Willum. He is lost."

For another moment they were silent, as men are when fatal words have been spoken; then the women's sobs burst forth.

"There's no time to cry—not fer us men, at least," added the father. "I've said my prayers, mother, an' you kin pray while we're gone. Dan'l, you go down to Brother Jake's an' tell him it was Willum's schooner that this man was in. He'd better take the boys an' go along the rocks west o' the beach. You come after me down to our P'int—no—you go with Brother Jake—I want t' be alone."

He walked away heavily, as one carrying a great burden. He could have no hope, but that worst assurance of death—the sight of death, of his son lying crushed and drowned on the rocks.

Mrs. Dempster went to the bed and, stooping over, kissed Mr. Waddy softly. The poor fellow, weakened by his hurts, struck to the heart by the sorrow he had brought to this family, burst into tears. And to mother and sister, also, came the agonising relief of bitter tears.

Mr. Waddy was left alone and, overwearied, he slept. And while he slept, life was busy with his frame, renewing it again, rebuilding all its shrines of saintly images, and all its cells where lonely thoughts dwelt sadly. When he awakes, his manfulness will avail that he may again take up the old burdens, which he had, in his dream, laid down.

All that day the father searched along the shore, seeking what he feared to find. He did not speak, but all the while his heart was calling upon one name; and there was no reply. He wandered along the jagged rocks of the harsh, iron coast, little coves and clefts interrupting his progress. Into every one of these he must peer shrinkingly, seeing in each, in a hasty vision of the mind, a form he knew, caught in the sheltered shallows and swaying heavily as the tide poured in over dyke of rock or strip of shining sand. He swung himself from crag to dangerous crag, recklessly—yet not recklessly, even in spots of desperate peril, but saving strength and untremulous vigour of hand and limb; for at any moment there might be for him a burden to bear, tenderly, lovingly, bitterly.

At times he would pause and look long and earnestly out upon the sea. The glitter of summer sunshine overspread its surface. Multitudes of brilliant sails, crowded by distance, came and went, and as they passed, he might imagine the cheery hail of whence and whither, and the wish from each to each of fortunate voyage. But his look did not rest on them; he was studying each hither surge, as it mounted and sank away—looking for something that was never heaved up by any sunlit billow, and that to see among the quick swoopings of seagulls would have been to him a horror and a shuddering despair.

Father and brother and kinsmen sought the lost in vain; while in vain the mother and the sister prayed as they waited tearfully. But there was no answer to their prayers, save that universal cruel one, "Be patient! Yes, be patient!"

CHAPTER VIII
MR. WADDY MUSES UPON FATE AND UNDERTAKES
A COMMISSION

THE family were all tenderly kind to Mr. Waddy, but he needed only repose. It was very sad within the house next day. Mrs. Dempster and Miranda made one or two attempts to talk with their patient, but his connection with the wreck was too close and too saddening. He brought their loss too clearly before them. They took refuge, cheerlessly, in household duties.

As the day advanced, Mr. Waddy was able to move about, and finally, dressed in Dan'l's clothes, to walk slowly with many halts down towards the rocks. Here he could sit with the breeze fresh upon him and basking in the bright sun. It was a very different heat to that dull, blasting one which had for years been trying to bake out all the lively juices of his system.

Cheroots were Mr. Waddy's favourite smoking. Of course he had none at present, after his wreck. Was it for the want of these that, even through his feebleness of a half-drowned man, his old impatience began to manifest itself? He had fancied, perhaps, that years of absence would have changed him from the hot, ardent, passionate, confident, and confiding youth of three lustra before. Were not fifteen years enough to stoicise and epicureanise him? Could he not keep cool and take his luxurious opportunities of a wealthy idler with passive content? Why must the native air awaken again the old thoughts and the old forgotten hopes? Forgotten! Ah, Mr. Waddy! hopes touched with disappointment may blacken into despairs, and pass into the background of shadow, away from foregrounds of sunshine in the heart, but there they must abide unfading.

Mr. Waddy, sitting by the seaside on The Island, was not merely impatient— an invalid may naturally be so when convalescence has made farther advance with his mind than his body—he was also very sad. He could not avoid connecting himself with the terrible disaster which had marked his coming.

"Just my luck!" said he to himself. "Why must I come home without any object? As soon as I arrive on this wretched continent, my passing at a hundred yards is enough to knock one boy into the water. Then I get myself left by the steamer, and to shorten my delay, I take the *Billy Blue Nose* and I become its Jonah. My vessel goes to wreck; my men are drowned: I am put under obligations to some romantic old maid, and then I have to make a whole family miserable with fatal news. And I am saved—for some good purpose I am willing to believe. But for what? Have I any duties besides to be a jolly bachelor and tell a boy or two, like that young Dunstan and his friend, how to behave? I believe I have not a relative in the world—save possibly that Mr. Waddie of New York—descendant, perhaps, of my Tory ancestor—who wrote me from Paris. It is rather pleasant to think of one relative, and then Dunstan told me that the old boy had an only child, a lovely daughter. Possibly she may be a cousin within the kissing removes. Ah, pleasanter still!"

Mr. Waddy was growing steadily more cheerful; then he fell a long time drowsily silent—dreaming undefined dreams—gazing out across the sea to the horizon, where wavering warmth of air mingled with quivering waves. But at last a chill in the air reminded him that he was still an invalid, and that evening was at hand.

"I must go in," he said, "and get ready for my start to-morrow. Dan'l must be persuaded to cede his clothes to me."

He went slowly back along the bushy path, pausing now and then to pluck a raspberry, until he came to the kitchen. He hesitated a moment, then went in. Everything was as before—the old clock ticking hours of a bitter day just as regularly to their end as it had marked hours of happy holidays, or of careful common days; the kettle of dried apples sputtering on the stove; the hot loaf ready for supper; Dan'l depositing the evening's milk on the dresser. But by the stove sat old Dempster, now doubly aged, stooping forward, his face covered with both his hands. Waddy hesitated about intruding his questions of business into the old man's grief. However, he looked up more cheerily than Ira expected, and giving him a broad gripe of the hand, asked of his health very cordially.

"I am so well," said Mr. Waddy, "that I hope to save you the trouble of keeping me longer than to-night."

"Make yourself to home," said Dempster. "You're welcome to stay as long as you like. 'Tain't in one day a man gits over bein' wrecked. Besides, I kind er like to have someone 'round; it keeps the women folks from thinkin' of their troubles. But if you'd oughter go, Jake 'll drive you over to-morrow, over to Loggerly."

"Yes," said Ira, "I think I must go. Is there anything I can do for you in Portland or Boston?"

"Wal, I guess I'll ask one thing; 'tain't much, an' you said my boy looked arter you a little, 'fore the schooner struck. There's a spot down on the sheltered side of Black Rock Head, jest to the end o' my meader, where I allers calkerlated to be buried, some day or other, along with the old woman. I can't find my boy to bury him there," he added simply, "but I'd like to put up somethin' of a moniment t' make us think of him. These gravestone pedlars don't come very often to The Island; they tried it fer several years, but folks seemed t' give up dyin' and they didn't git no orders. Wal, I wish when you git to Boston, you'd look 'round an' buy me a handsome pair o' stones, a big one with a round top fer the head, an' a small one fer the feet, an' have Willum's name an' age put on—I'll write it down an' Mirandy 'll look up a text. Have 'em leave room enough below Willum's for another name. When dyin' once gits into a family, there's no knowing where it 'll stop. I feel as if there'd be some more on us goin' afore long. They kin ship the stones in some of these coasters an' I'll pay fer 'em down to the custom house. 'Tain't askin' too much, I hope, mister?"

"Certainly not," said Ira, much affected and resolving that there should be no bill at the custom house. "I'll see that it is done just as you wish."

"Thanky kindly," said the old man. "When the stones come along, I'll set 'em under the cedars. It'll do mother an' me a sight o' good to see 'em an' kind er make our boy seem near."

"There's one thing I wish to speak to you about," said Mr. Waddy, after a considerable silence. "This Miss Sullivan—I have money enough and to spare. Do you know of anything I could do for her?"

The question was put rather awkwardly; Mr. Waddy knew as well as anyone that money is not the current coin to repay an act of devotion.

"Wal," said Dempster, seeing the good feeling that suggested and checked the inquiry, "I don't believe she wants fer money. She offered me a thousand dollars fer our P'int. I told her perhaps I'd sell out the whole farm for two thousand. I've been talkin' some, along back, with Willum, of goin' out west an' settlin' by some o' them big lakes. When folks has been used to water, they don't like to live away from it. Willum's gone, but Dan'l's a handy boy, an' Mirandy's as good as a whole drawin' of some men. I guess we'll go. It don't look quite so bright 'round here as it did," and he passed his hand across his eyes.

"If Miss Sullivan doesn't buy it, I will," said Ira quickly. "Can you tell me where she is to be found, so that I can have inquiry made what her decision is? This is just the spot I should like to buy—it is a good lonely place, where I can escape from my friends,—if I ever make any," he added, in a half-voice and rather bitterly.

"She came with a grist o' folks from York," said Dempster; "pretty good folks, but different kind to her. Mirandy had their names on a paper, but it got lost. But she said she'd write about the farm an' I kin let you know. Wal, if you want to go in the mornin' I must go over an' tell Jake. I'll be gone to the other field when you start; so good-bye."

He gave Waddy a crushing grasp of the hand and looked at him wistfully, as if he were recalling his son through this one who had seen him last. Then, feeling that tears—tears of that better manhood which men call unmanly—

were falling over his brown cheeks, now hollow with fatigue and sleepless grief, he unclosed his hand with grave gentleness and walked slowly away.

Looking after him, something brought back to Waddy's mind that sentence the old man had uttered a little while before:

"When dying once gets into a family, there's no knowing where it will stop."

He felt dimly that he had listened to a prophecy.

CHAPTER IX
THE NABOB RE-ENTERS CIVILISATION

IT was a lovely afternoon, two days after the events narrated in the last chapter, when a shabby stranger might have been seen slowly pacing the pavement that leads from one of those gates where a stream of ardent pilgrims disembogues into the purlieus of the Athens of America; pacing with reverent sloth up toward the Acropolis where, like fanes of gods still alive and kicking, tower the Boston State House, the Boston Anthenæum, and nobler than all, behind granite propylæa, the Boston Tremont House.

I said a shabby stranger might have been seen; he might, had anyone looked. But no one looks at shabby strangers, a fact for which this one was deeply grateful, for his name was Ira Waddy, and he was encased in a suit of Dan'l's clothes. He was still gloomy after his wreck, indisposed for the hospitalities of his commercial correspondents, not unwilling to visit his old haunts, himself unknown.

His first point was of course Dullish Court, his childhood's home; but it had changed beyond his recognition. Here, in place of the little shop, were the great Waddy Buildings, erected by his order and already trebled in value. The income of this unmortgaged property was of itself town house, country house, horses, dinners, balls, fashion and respect, the kingdoms of this world and another. Dullish Court had enlarged its borders for better perspective of these stupendous granite structures. Boston thought them more important than Mont Blanc, the Temple of Solomon, Karnac, or the Coliseum, and ciceroned the unsuspecting stranger thither.

"There, sir; what do you think of that, sir? We are plain, sir; but we are solid, sir—solid, sir, as the godlike Daniel said of us. All belong to one man. Boston boy, sir—went away with nothing; now worth millions!" and the liquid l's of that luxurious word dwelt upon the cicerone's tongue most Spanishly.

Mr. Waddy looked at his buildings with satisfaction. They were worth looking at. In them, everything that may be hoisted was hoisted; whatever may be stored was stored. Any man, from any continent or any island, would find there his country's products.

In front of the buildings were still to be seen sights familiar to Mr. Waddy's childhood, in other parts of the city. Here were girls pulling furtive pillage from the cotton bale; others making free with samples of everything from leaky boxes; others sounding molasses barrels with a pine taster and fattening on the contents. Mr. Waddy remembered his own childish days when a dripping molasses barrel was to him riches beyond the dreams of avarice; his days of growth, when as clerk, he became himself a Cerberus of barrels; his days of higher dignity when, Ira still, he, from his tall stool, was short with suppliants; and one more period of promotion when the inner counting-house acknowledged his services essential, and when Horace Belden, the ornamental junior partner, became his constant companion and most intimate friend, trusted with unnumbered confidences by the true and trustful Waddy. After that, came India and exile.

The shabby stranger moved on at last, rather content with his granite block, but regretting the old shop of his humbler days. The city was wholly changed. He recognised no building anywhere, but a vista of green trees appearing up a narrow street, he made for this. He came out upon the Common, and a very pretty place he found it, warm with rich shadows and all beflowered with gay little children. Fifteen years before, Mr. Waddy had sometimes done what may still, perhaps, be done by Boston swains and maids. He remembered circuits of the Common, transits of the Common, lingerings in the Common, by bright sunsets of summer, in electric evenings of frosty winters, when Boston eyes grow to keener sparkles, and Boston cheeks gain ruddy bloom; walks twilighted, moonlighted, starlighted—lighted beautifully with all-beaming lights of nature and youth and hope.

As Mr. Waddy, forgetting dinner, was gazing charmedly across the green slopes of this rus-in-urbal scene, remembering—pleasantly, doubtless, though his face did not look pleasant—his youthful strolls there-along, he saw sitting near one of the gates a miserable crouching figure, almost rolled into a ball. By its side was a box of withered cigars, and a placard, "Please buy something of this Chinaman." As Mr. Waddy looked abstractedly at him, quite certain not to buy, he saw a man of dark complexion approach the cringing figure, stare at him for a moment, jerk him violently by the tail, and then, with howls of joy chiming in melodiously with the other's howls of anguish, fall to embracing him ecstatically.

Mr. Waddy was much amused to recognise his servant Chin Chin in the embracer.

"What the devil are you doing with that chap?" he demanded, walking up and employing the toe of one of Dan'l's boots gently to interfere with this affecting scene.

"Hi yah! All same! Boston fashion!" shouted the delighted Chin Chin, recognising his master in spite of his disguise. "S'pose 'em drown. No! All same. Dis my cussem—murder's brudder's sum. Hi yah!" and he gave the cigar merchant another tug of the cue, another embrace, and a quantity of guttural gibberish. After this spasm of kinsmanly regard, he explained to Mr. Waddy that Dunstan had taken care of his effects and deposited them with a letter at the Tremont House, intrusting also him, Chin Chin, to the landlord's care.

Chin Chin, dressed in his neat uniform—Mr. Waddy would not call it a livery—seemed a Nepaulese ambassador, some Bung Jackadawr, on a visit of state, and Mr. Waddy his rough interpreter on savage shores. Some drygoods buyers at the Tremont House door were disposed to grin as the apparent Down East Yankee came up the steps, and to hee-haw when the landlord, recognising Chin Chin and the signature, asked the signer if he would like a private parlour. They grinned and hee-hawed no more when they caught sight of that name of power.

Meantime, Ira had been provided with his apartment. Chin Chin had arrayed him in a summer costume, easy and elegant, and he was dining vigorously, rejoiced to have someone near him again on whom his impatient oaths in Loo Choo and kindred dialects were not thrown away.

Of a large number of letters, he first opened Dunstan's. It was brief, merely informing him what had been done with the luggage. Mr. Waddy paused, however, over the closing sentences:

"I have a short hiatus in my life before the political campaign fairly commences, and shall yawn through it at Newport with Paulding. Why won't you drop in and see something of our world after your long absence? You will be amused and perhaps instructed in the new social discoveries. Your relatives, the Waddies, have a house there, a capital lounging place, and are expected back from Europe soon to occupy it.

"We made little Budlong rather unhappy for leaving you. Chin Chin shut off his cheroots. Miss Arabella wouldn't forgive him for abandoning 'that charming Mr. Waddy.' However, she consoled herself with Miromenil, that sprig of the *haute noblesse*. You will find them all at Newport."

"Fine lad, Dunstan," said Waddy, "but somewhat melancholy—probably spent too much money in Europe. Perhaps he's lost his heart to Miss Waddie; but he didn't talk like a disappointed lover; only sad, not bitter. Well, when I've finished my business here and Granby comes, I may as well begin my home experience with Newport—as well there as anywhere."

When the cobbler, being shaken, responded with only a death-rattle of dry ice, Mr. Waddy lighted his cheroot and strolled into the Common. It was loveliest moonlight. He sat on a bench reclined against an elm. The policeman coming by, stopped, willing to chat of crime. It was too pure a night for any thought save reveries of pensive peace; so Waddy gagged him with a cigar. An hour afterward, at midnight, the same, re-passing, found the smoker still posted on his bench.

So for hours of that delicious night of summer he sat beneath the flickering elm shadows. Sweet breezes from overland, where roses were, came and played among the branches. There was no sorrow nor sighing in the voices of this summer wind—only love, love! Did Mr. Waddy hear them? Had some hopeful Cupid peered into his face, he would have fled affrighted at its stern misery.

Across the ripples and beyond the silver islands of the bay, at Nahant, where one of the first hops of the season was now careering, the Wilkes party were spending a day or two. They were all hopping merrily to-night, Gyas the brave and the brave Cloanthus alternating with Miss Julia. Miss Milly Center had also been brought down to join the Wilkeses, by her Boston friends; and Mr. Billy Dulger, moth to her flame, had followed, disregarding the claims of his papa's counting-house in New York. They all danced and flirted and were well pleased, though not very susceptible truly to the exalting influences of the moonlit sea.

Miss Sullivan's dancing days were over, except when she was kind enough to practice with a débutante, or teach some awkward youth the graces in a turn or two. The music, however, was fine, and the girls, at first, fresh and not all crumpled. So she, too, was pleased with the pretty sight. But it grew no prettier, and presently she walked away from the hotel out upon the rocks. The music mingled softly with the plashing sea. The fall of waves was like the trembling of many leaves; each dot of water on the dark rocks was a diamond, filled with a diminished moon. Here, too, was the breeze that told of love; the lulling beat of waves said softly love, and the great, dreamy, mysterious sea, over all its brilliant and shimmering calm, seemed permeated by an infinite spirit of eternal love. Looking out upon it, Miss Sullivan's face softened and saddened, and her eyes filled again with tears.

About this time, Mr. Waddy, on his bench in Boston Common, feeling that the end of his third cheroot was about to frizzle the tips of his moustache, was taking a last, long puff, when a mosquito, suddenly sailing in, nipped his nose. The sufferer immediately discovered that his life was a burden. He threw away his stump with great violence, walked back to his hotel, and laid down his burden under a mosquito-bar.

CHAPTER X
OUR HERO RENEWS HIS YOUTH IN THE WARMTH
OF AN OLD FRIENDSHIP

AS Mr. Waddy was glancing over his paper at breakfast next morning, he caught sight of a name once familiar.

"Perhaps I did wrong," thought he, not for the first time, "to close all intercourse with people here when I went away. 'Perkins & Tootler' advertising everywhere. There can't be two men named Tootler. It must be my old schoolfellow. I'll go down and see if he remembers me."

Large letters in the directory informed him of the firm's address—Perkins & Tootler, wool merchants, Throgmorton Perkins, Thomas Tootler. Ira easily found the store. Everything looked busy and prosperous. The air around was filled with a fine flocculent haze which caused Mr. Waddy to rub his nose.

"Tommy doesn't need to advertise that he's in wool," thought he. "In clover, too, I should think."

All within the store of P. & T. was bustle. Wool-gathering there meant quite the opposite of witlessness. In reply to Mr. Waddy's inquiry for Mr. Tootler, a busy clerk pointed to the inner office. The door was shut, and as Mr. Waddy knocked, he heard a queer, suppressed sound, half musical, half melancholy, like the wheeze of a country church organ when Bellows, immersed in his apple, has forgotten his duty of blast.

"Come in," said a voice.

As Ira entered, the person within was engaged in hurrying something into the pocket of his grey morning coat. The person was a short, bald, jolly fatling, all abloom with pink freshness. He looked a compound of *père de famille* and jolly dog. His abiding rosiness was rosier now with a blush as of one detected; it grew ruddier as the stranger addressed him.

"Mr. Tootler, I believe?"

"Yes, sir; will you take a seat?" returned Tootler politely; then, as he saw his visitor in clearer light, he sprang to his feet, with hands outstretched. "Is it possible? Why, Waddy, is it you? *Folly ol tolly ol tilly ol ta!*" and he grasped Ira's hands and hopped before him in a polka step. As he hopped, his coat flew about and a hard object in the pocket struck Mr. Waddy's leg.

"Yes, it's I, Tommy, my boy," said Waddy, almost ready to dance himself and feeling, suddenly, quite a boy again. "I would bet cash that I can tell what you have in your right-hand pocket."

"Well, you're right," admitted Tootler, smiling blandly; and diving into his pocket, he produced the joints of a flute. He put it rapidly together and after one howl, such as Ira had heard from without, he played in a masterly way a few bars of a sweet Spanish air.

"Our last serenade—eh, Ira? I don't forget, you see."

The two friends shook hands again on this souvenir—but more gravely. Mr. Waddy's face, indeed, was again very grave.

"Fifteen years ago this very month," continued Tootler, a little rapidly, perhaps noticing the change. "But, Ira, you've not altered a hair, except your moustache, and you're as brown as a chowder party. Splendid! All right! Welcome home! as the boy said to the bumble-bee. If I could see your lips, I don't know but I would——" A chirping smack went off in the air, and Tommy, the gay, spun about his office, and as he spun he flirted no less than three tears to lay the dust; then, giving himself a little thwack in the eyes, he fronted Waddy again.

"Well, Tommy," said his friend, "you are the same—only younger. I see the hair hasn't grown yet on your infantile poll."

"Never will, sir," replied the merry man, who had plenty of pleasant light hair below his tonsure; "never would. I'm taken for a priest, a nunshow. Sometimes for the Pope. Isn't that worth being bald for? 'The Pope that Pagan full of pride'—I'd like to be him for one day to excommunicate the Irish nation. But come! tell me about yourself. I obeyed orders and didn't write. I heard, of course, through your house here that you were alive and making money, but nothing more. We've talked very often of you—Cissy and I."

"Oh!" said Waddy, "of course there's a Cissy. No man ever looked so young and happy without."

"Of course," assented Tootler positively, "there's more than one. There's Mrs. Cecilia Tootler, who knows you very well by hearsay, and Miss Cecilia Tootler, who will know you this afternoon, if my brown mare Cecilia doesn't break our necks."

"Where are we going so fast?" asked Waddy, "with these gay young men who drive brown mares?"

"We are going to my house in the country," explained Tootler. "We are going to drive and drive and talk over old times, and have some iced punch after the old fashion, and a pipe after punch. For your part, you are going to be made love to by Mrs. Tootler; she shall sing to you, with her divinest voice, everything that you have loved in old times, and a thousand new things that you will love when you hear them; she shall play to you on the dulcinea, sackbut, psaltery, spinnet, harp, lute, and every kind of instrument, including a piano. Her name was a prophecy—there's something in a name. Now yours—I don't believe you would have been bolting off to India as you did, forgetting all your friends, if your name had not been Ira."

"No more o' that, Tommy," protested Ira, "now that one of my friends has proved that he has not forgotten me. But tell me, is it usual for merchants of Boston, in wool or out of it, to carry pocket flutes or bassoons, and while away the noontide hour with dulcet strains, such as you gave me? Do they all play solos in solitude?"

"They might do worse, and some of 'em do. The fact is, Ira, I meet such a set of inharmonious knaves that I must soothe me with a little blow now and then. I have had the doors felted. Not much sound goes through. Generally, I can wait till I get to the Shrine—so I call my box—St. Cecilia's Shrine—for my music, but sometimes these confounded beggars rasp me so with their mean tricks and tempting swindles that I have to pipe up. The clerks wait till I've done and then ask for half-holidays. I have to deal with a pretty shabby crew. These manufacturers are always hard up and keep sending a lot of daggered scallawags here to get contributions to put little bills through Congress about the tariff. They don't get much out of Tommy Tootler—nor much ahead of him—the loafers!" and Tommy, to tranquillise his soul, took his flute and gave "Il segreto" with thrilling trills.

As he closed, a small knock smote the door and the youngest clerk, aged fifteen, peered in. His pantaloons were hitched up by his hasty descent from a high stool.

"Mr. Tootler," he began timidly, but gathering courage at every word, "my sisters are going to have a raspberry party this evening and—and my mother's not very well. Can I go home at three?"

"Go along, my boy!" said the merchant, "and don't take too many raspberries or you may be more ill than your mother."

Clerkling disappeared and a suppressed cheer came through the felted door.

Mr. Waddy laughed heartily. Tootler also smiled in length and breadth; in breadth over his rosy cheeks of indigenous cheerfulness, and in greater length from where his chin showed the cloven dimple up to the apex of his tonsure. It was doing Mr. Waddy vast good—this intercourse with his old comrade. It seems to me quite possible that if he had found his friend transmuted from the old nimble sixpence to a slow shilling—corrupted into a man of the two-and-sixpenny type, slim, prim, close, pious to the point of usury—that the returning man would have been disgusted away from all his possibilities of content and hopes of home; would have scampered back to the lounges of

Europe and there withered away. Then, certes, never would this tale of his Return have been written.

But Mr. Waddy found his old friend now even more a friend. The meeting carried each back to the dear days of youth, jolly and joyous, ardent, generous, unsuspecting. How many were left who could call either by prenomen? These were two who, together, had done all the boyish mischiefs—all for which boyhood is walloped and riper years remember with delight. Had they not together lugged away the furtive watermelon? What Boston bell-pulls were not familiar with their runaway rings? Who, as time went on, were the best skaters but they? Who went farthest for water lilies for boyish sweethearts; who, into stickiest mud for the second joints of that amphibious kangaroo, the frog? To enumerate their joint adventures and triumphs demands a folio. Were this written, the old types of friendship would be forgotten, and even now, as I think of Waddy and Tootler, those other duos of history, Orestes and Pythias, Damon and Jonathan, Pylades and David, mingle themselves like uncoupled hounds—their conjunctions seem only casual and temporary.

There must have been good reason for their reciprocal silence during so many years, for their meeting was not as of two who have wished to forget each other, and such a meeting, with so unchanged a comrade, was, as I have said, to Mr. Waddy a wondrous good. It seems impossible that a man of his many noble traits should not have had other friends, all in their way as sincere as this one. But whether this prove to be so or not, here we have the first fact a favourable fact. The first hand he grasps returns the pressure warmly, and not with traitorous warmth. The first face he recognises even precedes his in recognition. Pleasant omens these! If not ominous, pleasant enough as facts.

The two friends parted for their morning business. At three, to a tick, Mr. Tootler was at the Tremont House, in a knowing buggy with hickory wheels, fresh-varnished. Mr. Waddy, also to a tick, ready with his carpet-bag, squinted at Cecilia and saw that she was a "good un." Mr. Tootler, with his tonsure covered by a straw hat, was a very young, almost boyish-looking man, as vivacious and sparkling as a lively boy. Mr. Waddy was browner and graver, and his long moustache gave a stern character to his face, even when he smiled.

Cecilia lounged along over the stones down Beacon Street, with that easy fling which reminds one of the indolence of an able man. The air was cool and fragrant, and parasol clouds hung overhead, suggesting future need of umbrellas. The same need was foreshadowed by gleaming fires in horizontal blackness—they were evidently heating up those dark reservoirs that later a diluvial boiling-over might come.

Cecilia probably snuffed the approaching shower, or was a little wild with thoughts of her oats, for while Tootler was still pointing out to his friend the new houses of new men, the railroad causeways and the extension of the Common, the mare was imperceptibly and still lazily stretching into her speed. She was not one of those great awkward brutes that require a crowbar between the teeth and a capstan with its crew at either rein. This refined, ladylike animal had nothing of the wrong-headed vixen about her. Her lively ears showed caution without timidity. She was indeed a "good un," with a pedigree brought down by the Ark from Paradise.

Mr. Tootler hardly felt the reins, the mare was minding herself. They were descending an easy slope, when a man driving fast, alone in a buggy, appeared over the opposite rise of ground. Just as he came within recognisable distance, he struck his horse violently with the whip; the horse winced and bolted and then turned toward his own side a little, but not enough to save the collision.

"We're in," said Tootler calmly, as the crash came.

He had the advantage of down-hill impetus and a large fore-wheel of the new style. His wheel struck the other's hinder wheel just in front of the box. It swept the axle and both wheels clear. Cecilia pulled up in an instant—no damage. They left her standing and both sprang to the rescue of the stranger. He had been thrown out behind and was picking himself up from a spot where there was just mud enough for general defilement. Ira made after the horse, who only ran a hundred yards, and brought him back with the wreck of the wagon at his heels. Tootler was talking rather angrily to the stranger, who stood sulkily beating off the mud.

"Hang it, Belden, you know it was your own fault," said Tommy. "Why the deuce did you hit that bolter of yours just at the wrong time? You might have broken all our necks."

"Well!" said Belden, and the word expressed many things.

He was, or rather had been, dressed in white, with blue cravat, and wore a straw hat covered with fresh white muslin in the Oriental style. He was now bedaubed like Salius in the Virgilian foot-race. It was quite certain that his afternoon projects were at an end. He was an "object."

"After all," continued the good-natured Tootler, "you have the worst of it and I won't abuse you. Here comes Waddy with your horse—he seems all right. Don't you remember Waddy? Ira, this is Horace Belden. He used to be one of us—old friends."

Waddy was holding the horse with his right hand; he held out the other with an apology.

"I'm glad to see you again and very sorry that we were the unintentional cause of your accident," he said.

Belden took the hand with a bad grace, and stooping down to wipe off some of his stains, was muttering something that may have been a reply, when Cecilia made a little start. Tootler jumped to her head.

"Come, Waddy," he called; "we shall be caught in the shower. Sorry to leave you, Belden, but don't see that we can do anything. A little rain-water won't do you any harm."

Belden's manner was so very ungracious that Waddy's cordiality, if he felt any, was repressed. It was a case for indulgence, however, and he paused an instant as he was mounting into the buggy.

"I'm at the Tremont House, Mr. Belden," he said, "and shall be glad to see you."

"Tremont House—ah," replied the other. "Hold your head up, you damn beast!"

As the pair drove off, Belden looked after them with a black expression and a curse.

"What the hell has that damned Waddy come back for?" he asked of the ambient air. "He'd better keep away from me. I knew him as soon as I saw him from the top of the hill. You infernal brute, why didn't you go by?" and picking up his whip, Mr. Horace Belden beat his horse villainously.

Meantime Cecilia was tossing herself gracefully along, covering ground to make up for delay.

"Does Belden owe you any money?" asked Tommy. "I thought there seemed something to pay between you."

"He certainly didn't seem inclined to pay even common civility," replied Ira, "but I suppose he was savage at being spilt. It *was* rather hard, particularly with that gay and gorgeous raiment. He should learn how to drive."

"I think he knew us and meant to go by without notice," said Tommy shrewdly. "Did you ever quarrel with him before you went away?"

"Never any positive quarrel. I had begun to distrust him somewhat; but he aided me so readily in my efforts to be off that I forgot my doubts. We parted good friends. Why do you ask?"

"I can hardly say,—something in his look, and manner of speaking of you, as of course we did often. I noticed the same look to-day, when he used the whip, and when you came back with the horse. Depend on it, he wishes you no good. I don't like to speak ill of any man, but I believe him to be a scamp.

My wife would never know him. I ask her why, and she says she has an instinctive aversion to him. I am sure she has had something to verify her intuitions. She is not a person for idle fancies, except in my personal case, and then I had trouble enough to change fancy into fact."

"What has Belden been doing all these years?" asked Waddy. "The only time I ever heard of him personally was a year or so after I went, when a youth who came to China to forget some jilting miss, told me that he was to marry a lady at whose house we used to meet—you know," and he turned away so that his companion might not see his face.

"There was nothing in that," said Tommy. "Soon after you went, he ceased to be received there—reasons unknown. He was a pretty hard customer then, and played high. Then he got some reputation of a certain kind in an amatory way. By-and-by the house failed—total smash—not a dollar to be found; still his connections and power of making himself agreeable, particularly to women of the class who haven't intuitions, or don't consult them, kept him up. He's rather accomplished—sings, you know, and writes what half-educated people call clever things."

"He must have a large audience," observed Ira, a little bitterly, even for him.

"He has," agreed Tootler; "among knaves as well as fools. It's my belief the fellow would steal. In fact, where he got his money to go and live in Europe, as he did for several years, no one knows, unless he hid it from the firm's creditors. Then he went to California and pretended to have made his fortune. He has lately been to Europe again. I believe he is now on the matrimonial lay, the beggar! But you don't ask me about the other friends with whom we used to be so intimate."

"No," said Mr. Waddy, with the tone of one definitely putting aside the subject. "I do not. How that mare of yours travels! Can you put me in the way of getting a horse?"

"For what work? My next neighbour has a five-year-old, Cecilia's half-brother, for sale. He's a beauty, black as the devil. The only thing against him is, he's not broke to harness. They ask a loud price, too. It will make you stare."

"Not very easy to make me stare," said Waddy easily. "A saddle horse is just my affair. We'll look at him in the morning, and if he suits, 'Ho for cavaliers!'"

During all this talk, Mr. Waddy had not failed to observe the exquisite beauty of the country they were whizzing through. There is nothing so charming, suburbanly, as the region about Boston, and to him all was garden, for these were spots where his rosy-houred youth had taken its truant pleasures. Fifteen years had built fences of exclusion round many lovely groves, where he had chestnutted; the old orchards were cut down or neglected; many things had changed, for the city was steadily growing countrywards. He had only time to make hasty observations as they passed. Tootler would have been glad to pull up for larger view of fine house or finished grounds or lovely rural landscape, but that imperious shower said no. Presently they turned off the highroad into a sylvan lane, between tall hedges. A desultory avenue of elms shaded it. On one side was a gravel walk, along which a little girl was driving a hoop towards them.

"Jump in, Cissy," called Tootler, pulling in the mare.

A charming bright-eyed damsel clambered in and began to fondle her father. Her smile had the same bright, cheerful, magical charm as his.

"This is my friend, Mr. Waddy," said he. "Give him a kiss—or, better still, one for every year he has been away from his friends."

And again Mr. Waddy felt his heart glow with a warmth almost youthful as the fresh red lips touched his.

CHAPTER XI
IN WHICH THE READER IS ALLOWED TO WORSHIP
AT THE SHRINE

IF this were a three-volumed novel, here would expand a wondrous chance for a luxuriant, George Robbinsy description of that delightful rural retreat, the villa of Thomas Tootler, Esq. But though we enjoy the bliss and comfort of that worthy, we must leave his accessories to be imagined from the man. Of course he had a house, not too large, not too small for the pleasant actual trio of his family, and extensible to include future possibilities. Of course grounds were worthy of house, garden of grounds, fruits of garden.

The equine Cecilia walked slowly up the hill and lounged into the gate, no longer caring to hasten her certainty of oaten banquet, or spoil her appetite by trepidation. A fine-looking darkey stepped forward and took her head, while the gentlemen descended.

"Fugitive slave," whispered Mr. Tootler. "Jefferson Lee Compton Davis— first families of Virginia on the father's side and on the maternal grandfather's."

Little Cecilia had scampered away at once, and now reappeared, bright as a cherub in a sunbeam, leading her mother by the hand. At sight of the stranger, this lady checked herself at the threshold. But she had evidently, as Mr. Tootler said, heard already of Mr. Waddy, and when her husband presented him by name, she stepped forward with a shy tremble of diffident friendliness lovely to behold.

If Mr. Tootler had fittingly represented the masculine side of friendship, Mrs. Tootler as sincerely acted the feminine part. It was not merely the few cordial words, expressing her pleasure at meeting her husband's old friend, to whom he owed so much in so many ways, but the frank grasp of the hand, the bright look of genuine welcome in the clear brown eyes, the blush of warm interest, the winning smile as she introduced the friend into a home, as he must henceforth feel it—all this was more and more on the side of happiness. Mr. Waddy was again conscious of that unaccustomed feeling overcoming him, like a summer cloud full of summer's joyful tears.

Mrs. Tootler left them to give orders about the fatted calf and icing the champagne. Tommy conducted his friend to his room, and both, with their coats off, were commencing their toilet, chatting through an open door of communication, when there came a sudden alarm from little Cecilia.

"Papa!" she cried, running up the stair, "come quick! Some men are fighting Jefferson."

The host and guest were down the stair and in the barnyard in an instant. Four men were endeavouring to put the Fugitive Slave Bill in operation. Jefferson believed in the Declaration of Independence, and was making wondrous play for freedom, but four were too many for him. They had him down and were producing handcuffs. Two of the men were in the Virginia uniform of black dress-coat and shiny satin waistcoat. The other two were Deputy Marshals Hookey and Tucker.

It was beautiful as forked lightning to see Mr. Tootler count himself in and make free with the fight. He alighted like a bomb, unexpected, on one Virginian who had his knee on the negro's head. This man, for reasons, appeared no more in the fray. Ira, of course, followed his friend and occupied himself with raising bumps on the countenance of Marshal Tucker. Jefferson Davis, once released, soon floored the second Virginian.

"Cut, Jeff, and go to Sammy's," cried Tommy, amidst his attentions to Hookey. "I'll send your clothes in the morning," and Jeff was off in an instant.

The prey escaped, the two marshals preferred not to be bruised further and called a truce. Virginian No. 2 was quite groggy and *hors de combat.* Crackers, the dog, had pounced upon his fellow-huntsman as he lay, and was smiling at him with very white teeth. At this moment, with a neighbour flash, bang went the big thunder-gun and down came the deluge. The two gentlemen took refuge within, leaving the vanquished to scamper for their carriage with such speed as they were capable of. As the heroes re-entered the house, they met Mrs. Tootler rushing forward with a double-barrelled gun and silver fish-knife. The black cook, with a distinct cuisiney odor of fatted calf, was in the van, armed with a gridiron and pitcher of steaming water. This reserve was, however, needless as the Prussians at Waterloo, and there was no pursuit.

"Well, Waddy," said the host, "how are you? Knuckles lame?"

"No," replied the guest, "my man was rather cushiony about the chops. Neither of us was much hurt."

"Capital little shindy!" said Tommy, glowing with satisfaction. "I think I shall take a station of the Underground for the chances of such an appetiser now and then. I haven't felt such a meritorious hunger for ages. Very likely we'll be arrested in the morning."

Battles in a worthy cause win favour with the fair. Mrs. Cecilia looked a little anxiously for wounds, but there were none save what a stitch might repair. She plucked a rose for each, as a palm of victory.

At dinner, after the asphodel cauliflower, the lotus celery, the *pommes d'amour* tomatoes, and the amaranthine flower-adorned fruits, the friends talked over this mêlée, sipping meanwhile their nectar coffee, and wielding the nephelegeret sceptre of tobacco. Mrs. Tootler was not to be weeded out. They could not spare her presence, blithe and débonnaire, nor in the discussion her unembarrassed womanly rectitude.

"You must be indignant, Tommy," said Ira, "at the intrusion of those kidnappers."

"Unfortunately our moral sense on these subjects is too much degraded," answered Tommy. "I am angry, of course, but I do not think half enough of the infernal shame to that poor darkey. He must go to Canada, just as much an exile as any of the foreigners we make such disturbance about."

"I may seem rather ignorant," said Waddy, "after my long absence, but tell me, do men with the social position of gentlemen here accept office from a government that is willing to make and execute such laws as this Fugitive Slave Bill?"

"Why not? Mere social position does not make men gentlemen. They call themselves conservatives."

"It seems to me," said Ira, "that in the present condition of things, a conservative must be either an ignoramus, a coward, or a knave. But, madam," he added, turning to Mrs. Tootler, "we are boring you with politics. *Parlons chiffons.*"

"*Chiffons!*" cried Cecilia. "I am really indignant, Mr. Waddy. I do not believe that the gentleman so quietly smoking by your side would ever have been really roused if I were not always buzzing in his ears."

"She is right," admitted Mr. Tootler, sipping the last drops of his now cold coffee. "Women are vigorous antidotes to moral or mental sleepiness. But, Waddy, our little adventure is bringing the present too near us; to-night must be devoted to recalling our dear old days together. To-morrow we'll talk politics and be sad for the uncertainties of our cause—'ma quest oggi n' é dato goder,'" he sang.

"'Non contiamo l' incerto domani,'" responded Cecilia, with spirit, from the same air, "which I freely translate that we do not count the future of our cause uncertain at all, either to-morrow or after."

It is a fascinating thing to see a lovely woman in wrath, and probably Mr. Waddy thought for the moment more of how startlingly bright were the eyes of the lady, and how quick her heart's blood leaped to her vivid cheek, than of the cause that made the eyes electric and the cheek burning.

"My wife knows all the old songs, Ira," said Tommy, also gazing admiringly, but deeming it discreet to change the subject, "and I've not forgotten my stock. We'll have the old first, as old wine should come, and then, if satiety does not interfere, you shall have new music till you cry *basta*."

"Yes," agreed Cecilia, the little storm over in an instant, "I've learnt all your old favourites, Mr. Waddy. We have always expected you and determined to make you forget your sad absence," and then, as if she had been too frank and had betrayed some confidence of husband and wife, she shrank a little and folded into herself like a mimosa leaf.

"Thank you," said Mr. Waddy simply.

So they had music. Mrs. Tootler's voice was a pearly soprano of more marked tenderness and sentiment than you would have expected from her blithesomeness of manner. Tommy's was a barytone, strong and rich; it rolled out of the happy little man in a careless way, perpetually making musical ten-strikes. Mr. Waddy sometimes contributed a bass note, deep as an oubliette.

But it was his part to assist passively rather than actively at the concert. He would have listened quite forever, but at last the husband detected huskiness and said punch. Thereupon he brewed a browst—tumblers for the men, a wineglass for the lady. They partook by the rising moonlight.

"What are your plans?" asked Tommy. "You will stay with us a week, or a month, or five years?"

"I have no plans except to buy the black colt to-morrow. I expect pretty soon an English friend, and have promised to look up the lions with him. Apropos, perhaps you can put him in the way of seeing your Boston dons. He is an accomplished fellow, naturalist, man of science, charming companion, and brave soldier."

"He will find the Boston dons rather slow," said Tommy; "there is nothing soldierly about them. A respectably studious and rather dyspeptic set. Quite conventional and conscious of European influence. But here's to the midnight moon!" he added, as that gibbous deity cleft the clouds and seemed sailing upward through their stationary masses. "One can see almost heaven and the angels!"

"But why do you look up yonder for them?" queried Waddy, when the toast was drunk. "Your life seems to me a revelation of earthly heaven, with one abiding angelic presence. You think my rhapsodies mere Oriental absurdities, perhaps, Mrs. Cecilia—but it seems to me that my friend, with you, has attained to happiness. You were always a hopeful man, Tommy; now you seem by hopes achieved to have learnt what they call Faith. Well, you deserve it. For me, whatever I have deserved, there is only a poor refuge of such careless stoicism as I affect," and he uttered in some strange tongue an expression savage and stern as the growl of a lion.

"No!" said he again, after a silence, during which his friends had been, perhaps, seeking vainly for the right word; "my dear Mrs. Cecilia, my first evening at your lovely house shall not end sulkily on my part. Tommy, unsheathe your jocund flute and draw thenceforth soul-animating strains."

Tommy was not one of those non-performing humbugs, noticed by Socrates as existing in his time, who are uniformly out of practice or have left their notes at home, so he got out his flute immediately, and accompanied Cecilia in a delicious echo song, the silver sounds threading themselves among the fine moonbeams that floated through the network of vines over the piazza where they sat. With the last fading echo, drifted away every thought of bitterness, and the calm midnight silence fell around them peacefully. So they separated.

Mr. Waddy stood at the window of his bedroom, looking out upon the night. Was it to the spirit of the night that he stretched forth his arms and murmured words of yearning tenderness? His hand was feeling, as if unconsciously, in his bosom. He missed something.

"My Testament!" he exclaimed. "Ah, now I remember—the wreck."

He lighted a cigar, but after a puff or two, threw it away and turned in. His health was excellent, despite the memories which troubled him from time to time, and after the long day diversified with incidents of collision and shindy, he slept solidly, not far from the scenes of old happiness, lost long ago.

CHAPTER XII
THE PARABLE OF A HUMBLE BEAST OF BURDEN AND OF LILIES THAT TOIL NOT

BREAKFAST, with Cecilia to preside, was bright as summer sunrise. Little Cecilia had her bouquet of dewy roses for father and friend. The whiff of coffee perfume was like a gale of Araby the blest. Just as the meal was ended, a servant announced that Mr. Bishop was outside with a horse. They sallied forth to inspect it.

Mr. Bishop was a flashy man, not quite jockey, not quite farmer, rather of the squireen type. He had associated enough with gentlemen to know how they permit themselves to slang and swear. He was, however, better than a gentleman jockey, who, like a gentleman stool-pigeon, is doubly dangerous. But no jockey could say more for the black horse than was evident in every bend of his body, in every tense muscle and chord of the delicate limbs.

"He is high-couraged, sir," said Bishop, "and has played the devil with some folks. You seem to know how to handle a horse."

Waddy ran his hand over the legs, as free from knots as a Malacca joint; then standing at his head, he let the colt nibble at a bit of moist biscuit and took the opportunity quietly to look at his mouth.

"He seems all right," he said, at last. "Move him a little, if you please."

Bishop started him off. The stride and spring were smooth as a raw oyster; both told of speed and power.

"There's no mistake about him," said Bishop, bringing him back. "I meant to have kept him to ride myself, but times is gittin' hard [*i. e.*, brandy has gone up]. Besides, my daughter, Sally, is gittin' sicker an' I'll have to go south with her next winter and shan't need no horse, an' 'll want the rocks. Mr. Tootler knows the horse an' kin tell you what he did when we tried him on the course. If you buy him an' 'll keep dark, you'll be mighty apt to take 'em down that tries to run with you."

"I'll take him," said Ira, without more parley. "Tootler, will you give Mr. Bishop your check?"

While Tootler was drawing the check, Cecilia came out with a small basket. She offered it to Bishop.

"I've been putting up some jelly for Miss Sally," she said. "It may tempt her. How is she to-day?"

"The best to be said," replied Bishop, "is she ain't gittin' no wus. The doctor says she ain't so much sick as down in the mouth. She's off her feed an' seems to have got suthin' on her mind. P'r'aps it's religion. She wants me to stop swearin'; but I'll be durned if I kin. I wish you'd come over an' see her ag'in, ma'am. You're the only one as does her any good."

He spoke with evident feeling and sincerity, and Mrs. Tootler promised to go.

A moment later, Mr. Tootler emerged from the house and handed Bishop the check. The black was transferred to Mr. Waddy.

"I'm sorry to part with him," said Bishop, real regret in his voice; "but you look like you'd treat him well, sir. He ain't used to the whip. He's never been struck but once, when that damn Belden talked of buyin' him. Belden handled him kind er careless an' then give him a crack. I guess he got dropped easy—the fool! He's had a spite agin the horse ever since, an' I'm kind er glad to git him out o' the way of any mean trick. Belden's a kind o' feller not to fergit it when any critter's been too much fer him—horse or man or woman, either."

He looked at the horse for a moment, and then walked away, turning to look back once or twice regretfully, but consoling himself by the expensive check, subscribed by a man well known in State Street.

"Don't you remember Sally Bishop?" asked Tootler of his friend. "A very handsome girl she was—poor thing!—dying now. Seems to me you used to go with Belden to see her."

"I knew her slightly," replied Waddy, in a tone the reverse of encouraging. "It's a bad thing to have intimacies with second-rate women. If you have a saddle," he continued, "that will fit my horse, I'll ride him in to town now. By the way, what shall I name him? He's as black as death—'mors, pallida mors'—that's it—Pallid! I'll call him by rule of contraries. Pal, for short; we shall be pals, eh, old boy?" and he caressed the horse, who responded in kind, instinctively knowing a friend.

Pallid was larger than Cecilia, but her saddle was well enough for the short ride. Tootler was obliged to be in the wool again early. Jefferson Davis not being present to preside over the cavalry, the gardener laid down the shovel and the hoe and took up the curry-comb. Pallid was, of course, resplendent for the sale, as a bride is when her bargain is ratified.

Waddy was proud of his acquisition. Every fine fellow has something of the caballero in his nature. My friend, Misogynist, says a horse is the most beautiful animal.

"Woman! glorious woman!" I suggest enthusiastically.

"Good to look at," M. admits, "but bad to go. Be kind to the horse, and he is grateful and will not try to harm you. But woman—the more you let her have her head, the more she will try to throw you. Bah! my kingdom for a horse; he shall be king; no bedizened woman sovereign for me! Look at his smooth, brilliant coat—no pomade there! See that easy motion; *incedat rex*. Think of his simple toilet! two blankets, thick and thin. Yes, noble comrade! I will be no carpet knight, nor dwindle away with ridiculous sighs before shrines of plastic dough images, or of models of brassiness, but with thee will I away over boundlessness. Plains vast as the sea await our gallop. Charge!"

So far Misogynist—I will add that of the two classes of animals, horses are cheaper to keep, and when you have them, are yours, and not the property of the first admirer.

The gardener brought Cecilia to the door, shining from her morning toilet. Lady Cecilia, with the lesser lady, came to bid the guest adieu. Lady and child bore flowers of midsummer to be *rus in urbe* for the gentlemen. Cecilia was charming in her morning dress. As she said good-bye, the sparkle of her brown eyes was brighter, the blush warmer, the voice more musical, the shy tremor of friendliness more graceful. "Happy Tootler!" thought Waddy; "one of the rare few who are appointed to be illustrations to others of happiness."

"You will come again soon," said Cecilia. "A room in our house has become yours. You must inhabit it to keep ghosts from colonising. You too, perhaps, are in some danger of companionship of glooms, which are certainly as bad as ghosts. Come here always and we will sing them away. I have a dozen plans for you already for summer and winter—and then I intend you for a husband for little Cissy here. What do you think of it, Cissy?"

"I hardly know, mamma," said Cissy seriously. "I should wish to ask papa."

"Quite precociously right, my dear," commended Mr. Waddy; "a lesson to your imprudent mother."

"Not imprudent, Cissy," corrected Tootler. "You are wise to get the first refusal of our nabob. There will be hordes of matrons after him, like wolves after a buffalo, and they'll run him down unless he accepts his fate and consents to be shot beforehand. But come, Ira, I must voyage Boston-ward for the golden fleece."

"I go to New York this evening for a few days on business," added Waddy. "Good-bye, till I return. A kiss, little Cissy!"

Tommy said good-bye to his wife, and her bright smile went with him, as ever, and her glad voice sang about him in every silent moment of his busy day.

Mr. Waddy rode slowly along, trying Pallid through his paces. The beautiful head, unchecked by any martingale, shook and tossed in the freedom of a masculine coquetry. To control him was like managing the moods of a wild woman—charming distraction. Ira did not wish to trot him,—he was not to be a roadster,—but he gave Cecilia a little brush on a level. She was somewhere after the race, but it was lengths in the rear.

At the Tremont, Chin Chin was in waiting. The friends parted, and Mr. Waddy turned his face New Yorkward, in kindlier mood than he had known for many years.

That town, however, was not calculated to encourage moods of cheerfulness. He had seen others larger, several cleaner, many handsomer. It was hot, and mosquitoes were about.

Mr. Waddy's arrival was announced in the papers among "distinguished strangers." Old De Flournoy Budlong saw the name and called upon its owner in the evening. About matters personal to himself, Mr. Waddy talked little. He had not mentioned even to Tootler the incident of his wreck. But Mr. Budlong was too much occupied with his private affairs to question the mode of Mr. Waddy's arrival. The red silk pocket handkerchief of other days abode with him still, in flaunting defiance of the modern elegance of his family. In his talk, he used it freely on a forehead whose heated, anxious colouring might pale the cochineal of its polisher. He had much to say.

"Where are the ladies?" was naturally Mr. Waddy's first question.

"They are at Newport, sir," answered Bud, with a queer mixture of pride and apprehension. "They're at the Millard House. De Flournoy, Jr., is with them. It's very expensive, sir. Why, it's remarkable how that boy has to subscribe— five hundred dollars the first week! Subscriptions he says to the club and balls and picnics—I should judge he is very popular."

"No doubt," commented Ira.

"That Frenchman is with them, too," continued Bud. "What do you think of him?"

"Damned low beggar!" said Ira tersely.

Bud visibly brightened and polished himself in vigorous approval.

"Quite right," he agreed; "I respect your judgment, sir. I want Mrs. B. to drop his acquaintance; but she says he belongs to the hot nubbless, whatever that is. Why, sir, that Frenchman haunts me like a flea. Everything I eat tastes of frogs! And then Tim's subscriptions—five hundred dollars in one week! Why, sir, that would make him a life member and director of the Bible Society and the Tract Society and the Foreign Missions!" and the poor man fell to polishing himself again with his piratical handkerchief.

"I can't go to look after them before next week," he continued, "if then. You see, I've got a little operation in flour. It'll pay subscriptions, get him on the corn exchange, and Budlong is himself again. But it's dull music staying in town. I'm at the Astor. Everybody's away and there's no peaches," and old Bud, who had been working hard all his days, and now was more than willing to lead a life of jolly quiet, went off excessively disquieted.

"It's the old story," thought Ira, as he closed the door behind his friend. "I'm sorry for him. This is a case to put in the scale against Tootler. But it demands a whole cityful of Budlongs to over-balance one righteous man like Tommy and his family. Mrs. Tootler almost revives my faith in women, and I had thought that gone forever after that experience which nearly made my life a ruin.

"Rather a well-built ruin, though," he thought, glancing at the mirror, "and especially sound in the treasure-vaults. I would not quarrel with my experience for making me the man I have become, were it not that my isolation of bitter distrust in the one I most trusted has secluded me from all the chances of common happiness. And yet there are others sharing the same exile, bearing a heavier burden, who present a brave face to the world, even a cheerful one—for instance, Granby—married in a freak of boyish generosity to a vulgar, drunken termagant! Suppose I had fallen into the same mistake? Suppose I had married Sally Bishop; is it likely that I should have learnt to control the old Ira of my nature?

"All my voyage from Europe homeward, there was droning in my ears the monotonous refrain of a sad Spanish song, 'Se acabò para mi l'esperanza.' I heard it in the gale, the moment our schooner struck, and I thought 'now the old earthly hopes are dead with my death, and new hopes of other lives shall be.' As I lay in my trance, all the old bitterness passed away, and the old hopes grew fresh and confident again as in happy days before disappointment; and then the presence that was the joy of those days came near, and I seemed to have attained to dearest death and to a moment of heaven that should interpret all the cruel mysteries of existence. And I seemed to hear again the voice that flowed so deliciously through my youth and made my heart first know what heart-beats mean. But it was not death I had attained, only a vision, such as my waking life could never have, and when I really woke again in Dempster's house, it was to the melancholy of the same refrain, 'Se acabò para mi l'esperanza.'"

For a moment more he sat and stared down into the street with heavy eyes that saw not—what was it brought before him the face of Sally Bishop and beside it another face, her face——

He shook himself impatiently and cast his dark thoughts from him.

CHAPTER XIII
THE READER IS PRESENTED TO TWO CHARMING GIRLS, AND SO IS MAJOR GRANBY

AND now while a certain Peter Skerrett, stupendous wag, who is in town for a day or two and has been presented to Mr. Waddy by old Budlong, is showing the returned nabob through streets of deserted houses and telling him the necessary protective scandals about their owners:——

And while at Newport, in the society of De Châteaunéant, Tim Budlong is subscribing more freely than ever, and the Budlong ladies are quivering through the *ter-diurnal* shift of toilets resplendent:——

And while Sally Bishop, who has heard from her father how he had sold the black to a Mr. Ira Waddy, just returned from India, is dying with something on her mind which she dare not yet reveal:——

And while Horace Belden is beating his bolting horse and training another, to which he naturally gives the name of Knockknees, to run, and no doubt to win purses, and is nursing his finances for an August at Newport with its possible heiress:——

And while Miss Sullivan, at her lovely cottage opposite Belden's, is singing duets with Mrs. Cecilia Tootler, to whom, though that lady has often spoken of the delightful visit of Mr. Waddy, her friend, she has never yet mentioned her share in the rescue of a person of that name:——

While all our acquaintances are busied thus, Major Granby, at Halifax, boards a Cunarder, embarked for Boston. As he mounted the plank, a young excessively English man defended the gangway with open fist. The major won his entrance by grasping the fist in amicable guise.

"Why, how d'ye do, Ambient?" he said to his compatriot, a pleasant-faced pinkling. "So you have really started on your travels."

"Aw! Gwanby, I'm vewy glad to see you," replied Sir Comeguys Ambient, generally called briefly Sir Com. "Yes, I've begun my jowney wound the wowuld. It's lownger than I thought."

"You've had some pleasant company, anyway," said the major, examining discreetly two young ladies who stood near the rail, and who, seemingly, found much to interest them in the shoreward view.

"Yes; doosed handsome gerwuls," agreed Sir Com, "and vewy agweeable, but know too much."

"Not exactly in your line then, eh?"

"I'm weelly a little afwaid of them," admitted the valiant youth. "But the dark one is a wegular stunner for eyes and hair. The fair one is Miss Clara Waddie. The bwunette is her friend, Diana," and the pinkling's cheeks became all suffused with his ingenuous heart's blood.

"Ah," said Granby, observing the suffusion, "so that goddess—and she is a goddess—has transfixed you! Beware how you trifle with her; these American ladies do not hesitate to call a man out. Your Diana is divine, but your Clara is angelic. Waddy? I have a friend of that name. I'm going now to meet him in Boston."

In the course of the day, Major Granby, who had a soldier-like impetuosity in assaulting new opportunities, was presented to Waddie *père* and by him to the ladies.

Mr. Waddie of New York was a tall, slender gentleman, clean-shaven and high-cravatted. A bit of white collar on each side narrowed his range of chin movement. Dignity required that his head should not gyrate, hence sidelong glances were only effected by a painful twist of his eyes. He wore a blue frock, buttoned, and remarkably perfect boots. His manner was a little stiff, but entirely well-bred, and had a certain careful courtesy very attractive. Altogether, you would say, a man of limited, but not narrow mind, gentle and amiable. His passion was genealogy, and if he was ever querulous, it was when inevitable antiquaries connected him with the first Waddy, well known to all American pedigrees, cook of the *Mayflower* and victim of Miles Standish.

"Do I look," he would say, "like the son of a sea-cook, even in the sixth generation?"

And, indeed, he did not resemble a descendant of the caboose, but rather a marquis of the Émigration, such as we behold him at the Théâtre Français. This somewhat faded *élégant* had another passion: it was for his lovely daughter; nor was he the only man thus affected.

Mrs. Waddie was wifely, motherly, and a little over-energetic, as became the spouse of so mild and unpractical a gentleman. It was she who devised and carried out that purchase of real estate by which their comfortable property became a handsome fortune. It was she who officered the campaign which ended in giving him the civic crown of Member of Congress, and when the bad cookery of the American snob's paradise had impaired his health and compelled his resignation, it was again his energetic wife who suggested to General Taylor that she wished the embassy to Florence. It was obtained, of course, and was one of the most creditable acts of that President's brief career. His successor did not venture to recall Mr. Waddie, although he knew the scorn with which that gentleman, usually so amiable, regarded those ridiculously unsuccessful makeshifts and cowardly compromises of 1850. Mr.

Waddie's fortune, high social position, formidable wife, his serene worth and merited popularity, made him a person whom an accidental President could not presume to offend; and if he were already an enemy, at least it were wiser to keep him in a foreign land.

So his wife and the ambassador remained at Florence, where her balls crushed the Grand Duke's. She instituted a subscription for fronting the Duomo and introduced into Florentine life Buckwheat Cakes, Veracity, and Sewing Machines—of which only the first-named are still popular in that beautiful city.

It was the last year of the embassy when they thought proper to send for Miss Clara, who, with Diana, Mr. Waddie's ward, had been in charge of Miss Sullivan at home. This was the first year of Mr. Pierce's administration, and while he was hesitating whom to appoint in Mr. Waddie's place. He did appoint, in time, a tobacconist from the South-west, who viewed the world only as a spittoon.

Everybody has been in Florence or will go. It is not necessary, therefore, here to describe what Clara and Diana saw under the superintendence of Miss Sullivan, instinctive discoverer of the best. They were devout beneath the dome of Brunelleschi, rapt beside the tower of Giotto, critical in the galleries, gay in the Cascine. The Florentines adored Clara, the fair. Strangers worshipped Diana, the dark. This was not Diana, pale queen of night, but the huntress deity, bold and clear of eye, of colours rich and warm, with vigorous, fiery blood, hastening, almost fevering, a living life of passionateness. An Amazonian queen was Diana, who could do the dashing deeds of an Amazon with fanciful freedom. The Actæons dreaded her. No man of feeble manhood was permitted in her presence. Soldierly men and travellers she liked, and deep-sea fishermen, and blacksmiths and architects and heroes and lyric poets. And when any of these told her of his ambitions, large as life, or the dangers he had passed, and while he told, looked in her unblenching eyes and saw through them a soul that could comprehend any great ambition, or dare any danger; he, the strong man, always loved her madly. But she, the strong woman, the master-hero of her own soul, could not find her hero. There were ideal men in history for her to adore—at least, they seemed so, as history painted them—and as she read of them, she felt that strange thrill of despair for their absence that later she knew to be the passion of love—the passion of the woman longing for the fit, appointed mate.

The friendship of Clara and Diana was fore-ordained. Its historic beginning dates back to the college intimacy between young Waddie, refined, timid, studious, and Diana's father, a bold and ardent youth of southern blood and foreign race. This gentleman, being afterward unhappy in his home, wandered away into Texas. There he acquired immense estates by the purchase of old Spanish grants, and dying early, bequeathed his only child to his friend, Mr. Waddie, for care and nurture. The two girls grew up as sisters, and it was not until Diana's womanhood that the serious consideration of her orphanage was forced upon her. Mrs. Waddie, the kindest of mothers, was immersed in business, speculating for her husband, urging him forward to posts of responsibility he shrank from. She was therefore ready to yield her two daughters entirely into the hands of Miss Sullivan.

It was to Miss Sullivan that the task fell of telling Diana the sad history of her father and her mother, and how the mother, after a life worse than death, was now in a madhouse. It was a terrible revelation for this pure and brave young girl. In an agony of tears, she threw herself into Miss Sullivan's arms and prayed her to be a mother to the orphan. Miss Sullivan must have been of a nature singularly sympathetic, or herself have felt the loneliness of bitter grief, so deeply did she know the only consolations—endurance, and long-suffering faith, and hope in other lives, eternal ones.

Clara was present at this interview, and, after this, the relations between the elder and the younger women were closely sisterly. The elder sister, hardly older in appearance, except of paler and more thoughtful beauty, formed the younger minds.

Clara Waddie had inherited all her father's grace and refinement of face, form, mien, manner, and thought, and withal had gained from her mother judgment and strength of character, which underlay without diminishing her delicate sweetness. You might have known this fair young person for months and have given only a mental assent to her reputation of exquisite beauty; but one day, when some changing charm of emotion cast an evanescent flush upon her cheek and your sudden inspiration of eloquence had roused a look of interest in her lambent listening eyes, you would become conscious of more than mental assent to her unclaimed claim of perfect loveliness; your soul itself would thenceforth be cognisant of her beauty.

At the end of that delightful year in Florence, now rich with memories of the art and poetry of Italy, Diana was suddenly summoned to America. A most favourable change had come over her mother's malady, and with sanity returning, she was praying for kindly companionship and love. Her life, at best, was to be but brief, but it was thought that a residence in the dry, elevated regions of the interior might prolong it and allay the pangs of her desperate disease. Diana did not hesitate; she saw her duty clearly and accepted it, rejoicing.

Mr. Waddie went over with Diana. She found a mother with the saddened relics of a feeble beauty. Married hastily, out of silly school, she had been ignorantly, in her husband's absence, bewildered in the toils of a great villainy, which death to the villain and madness to the victim had sufficiently avenged. Rejecting Mr. Waddie's kind offer of escort, Diana took her mother to their estates in the up-country of Texas. In that most beautiful region, the Amazon could carry out her huntress fancies. She could gallop with her Mexican master of the horse over vast reaches of prairie, all her own. She could encamp in those belts of timber that sweep like rivers across boundless plains of Western wildness. At noon, when the deer she chased were hid in forest court, she, too, could seek such sylvan shelter, and lying there beneath an oak, all grey with mossy drapery, could take delight of dreamy contrast, and, with closed eyes, narrow her horizon with remembered palaces and rebuild under broad blue heavens the wonderful domes of Italy. Then she would study in some shady pool of the forest her face nut-browned to warm and healthy hues and fancy Clara, more palely beautiful, suddenly appearing, like Una from the ancient grove, and standing beside her at this softening mirror, as they had often stood in loving sisterhood before. In this existence, free and fresh, she learnt what so few women ever know, the pure physical joy of living.

The Texas postmaster was puzzled with strange stamps on Diana's constant letters from Europe; she was as constant in her replies. At last, she had sadly to tell her friend how her mother, after a sudden and fearful access of madness, had died. If there were any circumstances accompanying this death that made it doubly painful, and if, far away from the civilisation of towns, she had made other friends from whom this death was the cause of bitter parting, of this she said nothing to Clara. There are some secrets which honourable women do not impart to anyone more distant from their hearts than God. As to Endymion, it was certainly not probable that she had found him among Santa Fé traders, or Dutch emigrants, or rude cattle drovers whose best hope was a week of debauch in San Antonio.

She rejoined the Waddies and they did Europe. Mankind stared, and jealous women scoffed wherever Clara and Diana, charming pair, were seen. Diana was in mourning and very sad—sadder than seemed wholly natural for her mother's relieving death. The only gentleman to whom she allowed any intimacy was Belden. She told Miss Sullivan that she distrusted him and was displeased with the little she heard of his deeds, but that he was a bad imitation of an old friend of hers and she liked to be reminded of a favourite, even by a poor copy. I think upon this there must have been some very close confidence between these ladies; there certainly was a long interview, with tearfulness.

Are the Waddies of New York sufficiently introduced? We certainly know them better historically than Major Granby could, when, presented by Ambient, he had passed his first afternoon in their society. Not so well personally; one look of a practised eye discovers more than all description or all history can reveal.

Granby was a wide-worldling of the best type, and the ladies and Mr. Waddie found him charming. Sir Com Ambient, that pleasant pinkling of hesitant utterance, was also a favourite; indeed, Diana had quite petted him on the voyage, for she liked travellers, even verdant ones. Freshmen, when they are honest and ardent, are pleasant to meet. So she had petted him—poor Sir Com! He was not at all blasé, a fresh and susceptible youth; and of course he lost his heart utterly.

Granby spoke of his friend Ira. Mr. Ambassador Waddie had heard of this gentleman; in fact, who had not?

"We suppose Mr. Ira Waddy to belong to a younger branch of our somewhat ancient family," he explained. "Indeed, I have already written him to inquire our relationship. We shall be happy to meet him as a kinsman and as a friend of Major Granby."

The young ladies were interested in the major's account of his friend. He was not, Granby said, a misogynist, though he always avoided women if he could. He was a cynic of the kindest heart. Utterly careless of money, but possessed of a Pactolian genius for making it, he dashed at a speculation as a desperate man rides through a front of opposing battle. It seemed that he valued success so little that the Fates were willing to give it him.

"Perhaps," said Diana, "the Fates took an antecedent revenge. Perhaps they are lavishly compensating him with what he does not value for the fatal loss of what he did."

Granby looked hard at her, studying the hieroglyphs of her expressive face. What experience had this young person had, enabling her to divine such secrets of his own life and what he had divined in his friend's history? A sham Champollion would have given his interpretation that she was generalising from some disappointment of the wrong man and not the right one having offered her a bouquet. Granby, looking deeper, perceived that to this maiden, whom the gods loved, they had given some early sorrow, which she was endeavouring to explain to herself.

Granby went on with the character of Mr. Waddy. He was a man who concerned himself not much with books. Having his own thoughts, he did not hungrily need those of other men. He could exhaust the books by a question or two from those who took the trouble to read them. But if generally not a believer in the works of men or the words of women, he was a child of nature.

"During the long and excursive pilgrimage from India to London," explained Granby, "which we have made together, there is hardly one oddity, one beauty, one fact or phenomenon in nature, not human, that we have not investigated. We've shot and bagged everything; we've fished and fished up everything."

And then, the major, who liked to talk—and who does not?—to beautiful women, told them snake stories and tales of crocodiles, and how, in the primary sense, he and his friend had seen the elephant and fought the tiger. Then he passed to the Crimean campaign, where Mr. Waddy had joined him and gone about recklessly to see the fun of fighting and relieve its after agony. On the side of fun, there was a story how Mr. Waddy and Chin Chin had surrounded a picket-guard of a Russian officer and four men and brought them in prisoners at the point of their own bayonets—a pardonable violation of the neutrality laws. On the other side, was the account of Major Granby's own rescue by his friend. Granby told this last with an enthusiasm that showed the earnestness of his friendship.

The two girls, who would have given up life or a lover, one for the other, felt a romantic interest in the alliance of these men, both apparently isolated, and erratic for some good cause from tranquil happiness. Diana's interest was that of a comrade in these adventures; Clara's was an almost timorous sympathy. Ambient listened and blushed pinker with excitement. He was a little cut out by a man who had done what he only hoped to do; but Sir Com was a good fellow, and while the first fiddle played, he put up his pipe of tender wild oat in its verdant case and applauded the solo heartily.

By Mr. Waddie's invitation, Granby and Ambient joined his party at the Tremont House. The ladies also suggested Newport, whither they were all going. Granby mentioned his half-engagement with Mr. Waddy to drop in at that watering-place on their tour, and said that the pleasure of their society, etc., etc. In short, if he could persuade his friend, they would drop in, and "we'll give you a plunge, too, Ambient," he promised.

This conversation took place at the breakfast table, the morning after they landed. The ladies presently disappeared and, when they reappeared, were resplendent with results of unpacking. The proud and brilliant Diana was still in half-mourning. I think this Amazon must have beheld Clara's loveliness with almost masculine admiration and have expressed it with manly compliments, for Clara seemed a little conscious as they stepped into a carriage, not quick enough to avoid the two gentlemen. These knightly squires were eager for a glimpse at brightened beauty. Granby assumed the privilege of handing them into their go-cart, while the humbler Ambient defended skirt from wheel.

"We are going," said Diana, "to pass the morning with our friend, Miss Sullivan, in the country."

"Adieu the eagle and the swan!" cried Granby, as they drove off. "By Imperial Jove! Ambient, she is worthy to be the consort of a god. If I was ambitious, as you are, I should aspire as you do and as much in vain. I suppose this is your first love, eh? You're luckier than most men. A man's first is generally either a grandmotherly old flirt become *dévote*, or some bread-and-butter, sweet simplicity,—oh, bah!"

"Lucky!" echoed Ambient. "I'm confoundedly unlucky and unhappy. She'll never have anything to say to me—except in that infernal condescending *de haut en bas* style, as if I was a boy. I'd like to pwove it on somebody that I'm not!" and Sir Com looked around with a quite fierce expression upon his pleasant countenance.

"Well, I'm not at all sorry for you," said Granby cheerfully. "It never does anyone any harm to be desperately in love with a woman who is worthy. You may be sure that Diana will never flirt with you."

"She fluriot!—she would never care enough for anyone's admiration to twy to gain it. I only wish she would fluriot with me; then I could be angwy—now I'm only wetched."

"It will not help you to know that everybody must go through it," said Granby, his face grave again—even a little bitter. "I have, my dear fellow—and worse. For my part, I admire the goddess immensely; but I think I could love her friend more—that heavenly mildness gently soothes my soul. The nose," continued the major, waxing eloquent, "is man's most available feature—it may be tweaked. The mouth in woman is delicately expressive and available when we are allowed to"—and he raised his fingers with courteous reverence to his lips. "But the mouth is external merely. Who wishes to look down it, even though heart may be in throat and panting at the parted lips? It is the eyes—eyes like Clara's, where there is soul beneath the surface and down in the deep profound of those wells of lightsome lustre is truth—these we may dreamily gaze in for life-long peacefulness."

Ambient stared at this rhapsody, not quite certain whether his companion was in earnest. But before he could decide, a carriage drove up, and Granby gave a distant view-halloo as Mr. Waddy stepped out.

"Punctual to a tick," said Ira, holding up his watch and producing the rhinoceros-horn match-box and his case of cheroots.

Granby took one, presented Sir Com, and they entered the hotel together.

Horace Belden was out that morning exercising his race-horse Knockknees. As he descended the same slope where he had fouled with Tootler's buggy, he saw approaching a carriage with two ladies. He recognised them instantly, with a leap of the heart. He drew up by their side with polite commonplaces of welcome, dashed with more meaning when he addressed Diana. They told him whence and whither—to-day to Miss Sullivan, to-morrow to Newport.

"How can you like that man?" asked Clara, as they drove on. "He seems to me a Sansfoy."

"I do not like or trust him," replied Diana. "I tolerate him because he rides well and is agreeable, and because he reminds me of an old friend."

She stooped to pick up a broken-winged butterfly that had fluttered feebly into the carriage. Stooping sent the blood into her face. While they cherished the poor insect, she grew of a sudden deadly pale, and putting her hand to her side, shuddered slightly. Clara did not observe the motion, which was not repeated.

There is no need to describe the meeting between pupils and preceptress; but in the late twilight Clara returned without Diana, who had consented to stay a day or two with Miss Sullivan. She wished to keep both the friends, but Mrs. Waddie would need her daughter in arranging their house.

Mr. Ira Waddy lionised Boston with Granby and Ambient. They looked in for a moment on Mr. Tootler. He was composing an air to a Frémont song which he had just written, and which Mrs. Tootler would revise—and perhaps infuse with even sharper ginger. He played it for them on the flute. Sir Com listened with astonishment. Mr. Tootler figures in the chapter entitled, "An Hour with a Musical Wool-Merchant," in that young gentleman's book, "Pork and Beans; or, Tracks in the Trail of the Bear and the Buffalo."

In the evening, Waddy and Waddie became acquainted. The ambassador accepted the relationship, which was now fully established by relics and traditions. The Great Tradition, however, of the *Mayflower*, the caboose, Miles Standish, the pepper-pot—this he laughed at as legendary. Ira clung to it vigorously; he liked to have come in with the Pilgrims, even at the expense of humble ancestry and an inherited curse.

The serene Waddie, whose life was happy gentleness, whose toil had been done for him by fortune and by feminine energy, had no occasion to look to the past for causes of present exasperating characteristics. He had inherited the family mildness, and though he decorated his social station, he was not one to have assumed it. He acknowledged his obligations to his wife. He had thus ignorantly fulfilled the destiny of his race.

Clara gave the legend her full adhesion; but nothing was said in this conclave of the Tory sutler, or the Revolutionary sergeant.

Diana was missed, but the name of her hostess was not mentioned. There was no reason why Miss Sullivan should be talked of among strangers; no one knew of that incident of Mr. Waddy's Return where she had appeared and played so important a part, nor that he would be pleased to see and thank his preserver.

In the morning, the whole party went to Newport. Thither all the actors of our drama are centering. It is strange by what delicate links of influence life is bound to life—what chances of seemingly casual meetings and partings determine history!

Pallid went with his master; also a fast pair that Tootler had purchased for Mr. Waddy, who meant to be both charioteer and cavalier.

CHAPTER XIV
PROTECTIVE SCANDALS AND OTHER DIVERTING HUMOURS
OF A FASHIONABLE WATERING-PLACE

ONCE upon a time, by a chance of history, a small man was thrust into greatness of place.

Moulded in putty for a niche, he tottered and crumbled on a pedestal.

This pedestalled weakling, small in his great place, prayed for support. He got it on conditions—rather shabby ones. He was to acknowledge himself frightened, his niche in life a mistake. He was to deny his old views of right, and compromise away right for a novel view of ancient wrong.

When time came that he should remove, he was willing to stay and be a dough image in a high place; but a grateful people of a grateful republic did not invite him.

At another time, a grateful people rather scornfully declined him a re-invitation to the old place, though he prayed it in suppliant guise.

But a grateful people did as much as could be expected; they built a great hotel at Newport and named it by his name. It still lives, and its name is "The Millard."

What they call the odour of respectability that hangs about an old institution is not always fragrance when that institution is a hotel. There, most people prefer the odour of new paint. So it was with our dramatis personæ. They chose the Millard, not from sympathy with its name, but with its newness.

Mr. Waddy preferred going with Granby and Ambient, whom they had adopted, to abandoning these friends and accepting the invitation of his ambassador kinsman. So these three gentlemen inscribed themselves upon the books of the Millard.

Miss Arabella Budlong had just returned from her bath. She was in the hair and costume of La Sonnambula in the bridge scene, and it was a little dangerous, her rush to the window to inspect the companions of Mr. Waddy. She might have been seen—in fact, she was seen, but not recognised, by Peter Skerrett, who had arrived that morning. He called Gyas Cutus and told him to look at Venus Anadyomene, drying herself in the sun.

"Anna who?" asked Gyas. "That's Belle Bud. She's always drying at this hour, and I believe doesn't care who knows it. I say, Peter, who are those chaps just come in? You know everybody before he is born. A very neat lot they are."

"That brown one with the cheroot is Ira Waddy," replied Peter, "the partner of the great East Indian banker, Jimsitchy Jibbybohoy. The big man is the Grand Duke Constantine, come over to study our institutions, republican and peculiar, with a view to the emancipation of serfs. Number three is the eldest hope of the Pope."

"Gaaz!" said Gyas, with indescribable intonation. "The Pope don't have eldest sons."

"I would be willing to have him the old gentleman's youngest to please you," replied Peter, "but historic truth is a grave thing. Apropos of boots and kicking, I significantly advise you not to call that young lady Belle Bud any more."

Misses Julia Wilkes and Milly Center were in the Millard parlour with Cloanthus Fortisque and Billy Dulger. They saw the stranger gentlemen arrive, and Milly felt her *volage* little heart expand toward Ambient, that rosebud of Albion. She had a lively imagination for flirtations and immediately built an ideal vista with a finale of a kneeling scene, Ambient, in tears, offering his heart and a dukedom. She was not quite decided whether to raise him from his entrancement by a tap of fan, as wand, or to leave him in that comical position and call in a friend to witness her disdained triumph.

"Go, Mr. Dulger," said Milly, with the despotism of a miss in her position, "and find out who they are—particularly that handsome young man in the curious coat, lovely complexion, and mutton-chops. He looks so sweet."

Poor Dulger, compelled to prepare the way for a possible rival, went off savagely.

"I'll make her pay for all this sometime," he murmured, with clenched fists.

Dulger was fast getting desperate. He had been with this young fair one a centripetal dangler or gyroscope for years. Milly had taken his bouquets all her winters, without regard to expense. But other bouquets she had likewise taken, to the dismay of his faithful heart. When cleverer men, or bigger men, or men with more regular features or less sporadic moustache, came, yielding to Miss Milly's seducing attentions,—and she was not chary of them,—poor Dulger sat in the background, looking at his tightish new boots, and bit his thumb at these cleverer, bigger, handsomer. He could not understand the world-wide discursiveness of the clever men, nor in truth, did Milly, but she had tact enough to see when her locutor thought he had said a witty thing, and then she could give a pretty laugh; or when it was a poetical, sentimental thing, she could look down and softly sigh. A man must have flattery for his vanity as much as sugar for his coffee, and Milly was very liberal of that sweet condiment. Her charm lasted with the clever men days, weeks, months, according to their necessities for unintelligent flattering sympathy and the frequency of their interviews.

Billy Dulger had seen so many generations of such lovers come and go, more or less voluntarily, that he began to feel a pre-emptive, prescriptive, or squatter sovereign right to the premises; for there were premises, as well as a person—a house where one might willingly hang his hat. Miss Milly was an orphan and had a house—nay, many houses—of her own. Her lover was proceeding in the established manner of courtship by regular approaches and steady siege. It generally succeeds, this method, and is, after all, easier to the dangling man of no genius and safer than the bold assault of a hardy forlorn hope. So many campaigns—such constant cannonade of bouquets with great occasional bombardment of flower-baskets—missives proposing truce—shams of raising the siege—showers of Congreve rockets in the form of cornucopias of bonbons—parleys of no actual consequence effected by sympathising allies—cautious spying with lorgnette, followed by assault upon opera box—watchful pouncings when the garrison sallies forth for stores—patience, pertinacity, and final success: this was Mr. Dulger's game. It was, however, no sport to him. It cannot be sweet for a man to be forever in the presence of a woman he loves or wants, he playing the triangle while a *gran' maestro* is leading at the apex of the orchestra. He cannot enjoy hearing her applaud another man for saying things he cannot possibly think of and does not quite understand. Billy, therefore, was not happy in his courtship. He knew his love was a flirt, and not particularly charming, except that she made a business of being so. But it had become with him a vice to love her, if such is love. Should he ever succeed, after his ages of suspensory dangling, he will not be brilliantly happy. This is experience which he will remember, and though a well-enough intentioned man, he will necessarily avenge with marital severities his ante-nuptial pains.

Have we dallied too long with Miss Milly and Master William? They are essentials in this history, and, though casually as it would seem, yet on them depends its event.

As Mr. Waddy turned after booking himself at the Millard, he found his hand suddenly seized by Mr. De Flournoy Budlong. The bloom on this gentleman's cheeks had jaundiced to autumnal hues. His smooth, round, jolly face had shrunken and was veined with dry wrinkles like a frozen apple. Poor Bud, flowering no longer, seediness was overcoming him, to no one's special wonder who saw the principal female of his family conducting herself very much indeed, and watched young Tim subscribing every night.

"Glad you've come," said Budlong, with unhappy cordiality. "I got here this morning. Peter Skerrett said it was time for me to be on hand and gave me half his stateroom. Seasick all night; yes, sir, every minute. Peter says juicy men always are. Deuced rough off P'int Judith. Peter said it was the story in the Apocalypse, Judith, and whole infernos. Found Tim with his head very much swelled. Bad cold, he said. I told him he'd better stay in bed. He said he would till evening—had a small subscription party at nine. Asked him to take me—he said strangers had to be balloted for once a week for three weeks. I'm afraid it's all poppycock. Mrs. B. has gone out to walk with that blasted Frenchman. Ah, here she comes now."

Mrs. Budlong entered with Auguste Henri. She dismissed her escort with a whisper and walked up to her husband, very handsome, very well dressed, perfectly at her ease, and gave him two fingers of the hand which held her parasol.

"How d'ye do, pa?" said she. "You've left us to take care of ourselves so long that we thought you'd forgotten us. I'm sorry you didn't let me know you were coming; you could have brought up another horse instead of Drummer."

"What's happened to him? He's my best horse," said the husband thus tenderly received as master of the cavalry.

"De Châteaunéant was riding him, and that rude young Dunstan, driving the Wellabouts, ran into him. Drummer was badly cut and Aug—De Châteaunéant had his—his clothes torn. He intends to punish Dunstan, who was very insolent."

"I hope he will," said De Flournoy, rubbing his hands and brightening up. "I should like to see the beggar well thrashed"—of course it was Dunstan he meant.

Mrs. De Flournoy had been quite conscious of Waddy's presence during this colloquy. Waddy was a man whom she was willing to propitiate. She had even tried her fascinations on him early in the voyage—merely in the way of a flirtation, of course. But Ira was loyal, though not pretending to be a saint, and remained impervious to the darts which Mrs. B. shot at him from her expressive eyes. To Ira, therefore, Mrs. B. now turned, bowed gracefully and smiled pleasantly. She had the spoiling of a very fine woman in her.

"We were sorry to be deprived of your society on board," said she, with easy suavity, "even for so heroic a reason. We were hardly willing to speak to Mr. Tim Budlong after his abandoning you. But he is so aristocratic. He said he thought the little beggar might as well drown. We, of course, did not think so. I hope to see you often while you are here. We will study American society together. One of the charms of hotel life is that we can see our friends so constantly and familiarly and form agreeable intimacies."

All this was said in Mrs. De Flournoy's most gracious manner to Mr. Waddy, and at him and his friends. She was determined to make a good impression—excessively determined, unfortunately. She wished to signalise her first summer after Europe by great social triumphs and courted everybody, except those whom she could venture to contemn. Still, men at a watering-place are not disposed to reject the advances of pretty women, and Waddy would have been placable, but that he did not care for intimacy with a person who could accept De Châteaunéant as *cicisbeo*, or even acquaintance. He could not forget signs of a complete understanding he had detected between him and the lady. However, Waddy said the civil nothings and Mrs. Budlong went upstairs, followed humbly by poor old Bud.

Peter Skerrett calls the stair at the Millard "Jacob's Ladder," because, says he, "the angels who have good tops to their ankles are continually ascending and descending." Up Jacob's Ladder, then, Mr. Waddy and his friends presently marched to their rooms.

When the trio, after their toilet, descended, they found the hall lined with people awaiting dinner. Peter Skerrett stepped up to greet Mr. Waddy.

"Come, Peter," said the young nabob, introducing his friends, "sit down and tell us what you call the protective scandals. We are all green at Newport."

"That is a new expwession to me," said Sir Com, gaspingly as usual. "Pwotective scandals—what does it mean?"

"Strangers," explained Peter oracularly, "before they are up to trap, are apt to put their foot in it. They need someone to inform them who are the people they must know, whom they may know, whom they may know under penalties, and whom they must not know. They need also a general guide to conversation—to know to whom they shall say, 'Man is the architect of his own fortunes,' and to whom, 'It is a noble thing to be descended from a long line of proud and noble ancestors.'"

"Must we learn the pedigwee of evewybody here?" demanded Ambient, in consternation. "I shall have to cwam like a fellow going up for his gweat go."

"Ah, there you've hit it," replied Peter. "The actual pedigrees are almost none, thanks to republican institutions. Except a very few families, who have managed to hold together and keep pelf to their names, there are no pedigrees to remember. As a Nation, we have buried our grandfather. Parentage only of everyone is what you must know. We are a religious people," and he turned his eyes upward whither the ceiling was between him and heaven, and motioned as if to cross himself. "Yes, fervently religious, and have read in Holy Writ that labour was a curse. We have agreed that it ought to be expunged. But as it is almost impossible in general powwow to avoid alluding to some trade or business, the great protective scandal is to know the individual one not to mention to each of these people. They do not wish to be reminded by what especial class of curse their papas were made miserable and millionaire.

"For example," continued Peter, delighted to have the floor and so select an audience, "that rather long girl, walking with a race-horse stride, is Miss Peytona Fashion. Her parent began his fortune by betting against his own horse. It would be deemed uncivil if you, Sir Comeguys, should stand before her, and with a whiff at her circumambient atmosphere of odours, should ask her if her favourite perfume was Jockey Club.

"So there is hardly one subject that is not taboo with someone. Mrs. De Flournoy Budlong loves not to hear of flowery meads or breakfast called a meal—it seems to let the cat out the bag. Old Flirney, you know, began as a deck-hand on a barrel-barge, and has, turned to the wall in a lock-up in his garret, a portrait of himself shouldering a cask of flour; that portrait is her closet skeleton.

"Ah, I see you have spotted the Southern belle," added he to Ambient, who was gazing at a dark, luxurious beauty opposite him.

"Spotted her!" echoed the youth, blushing pinkly. "I wouldn't do it for the wowuld."

"Oh, I mean remarked her. You'll learn the language by-and-by. You're looking at her foot—that's the pretty one; the other's enlarged in the joint by dancing. Well, that is Miss Saccharissa Mellasys, the creole belle from Louisiana. You're an abolitionist, I suppose?"

"Yes," said the Englishman: "isn't evewyone who has no pecuniawy intewest in slavewy?"

"Of course," replied Peter, "more or less so. But beware of talking anti-slavery to Miss Mellasys. You'll bring an unhandsome look into those tranquil eyes. She's here on the proceeds of one of her half-sisters. Success of abolitionism would knock off her summer trips to civilisation, and she knows that her amiable papa wouldn't hesitate to sell her, as he does the scions of his dusky brood, without too much inquiry as to the purpose."

"You call this a democratic republic, I believe," said Granby.

"'Tis the land of the free and the home of the brave!" cried Peter, waving his hat. "Pardon this ebullition of national pride. I'm getting up my enthusiasm for a presidential stumping tour this fall. Well, Saccharissa is very pretty. I'm told they cultivate that startled expression of the eyes at the South by placing the girls, when they're infants, on the edge of a bayou; the alligators come and snap at them, but the nurse runs them off just in time."

"Will you allow me to make a note of that custom?" asked Ambient, who had listened open-mouthed.

"Certainly," assented Peter graciously, "and I can tell you more of the same sort, if you wish," but the sound of the dinner-gong prevented further recitals.

Tim Budlong appeared at dinner, all beauteous with raiment, but looking desperately roué. He had, too, the peculiarly anxious look of an amateur subscriber, so different from the cautious carelessness of the professional receiver of subscriptions.

Tim was disposed to dodge Mr. Waddy; but Ira had no quarrel with the hopeful youth, who had in the Halifax affair only done as most men do. It is not worth while, as Mr. Waddy knew, to be permanently disgusted with human beings for acting according to their natures; he knew that character is a compound of blood, breeding, and experience. So he gave Tim a glass of claret and said "*Pax vobiscum*, my lad!" very kindly.

Tim, pleased with the patronage of the distinguished stranger, who, with his two friends, and Chin Chin behind his chair, was an object of gaze at the Millard—Tim, elated by such good society, for twenty minutes resolved to reform. At the twenty-first minute, he caught a wink from Gyas Cutus, and with a knowing crook of the elbow, turned off his glass of what Millard called champagne and became a reprobate again.

After dinner, Peter Skerrett was besieged by speculators for information. "Who are your friends?" was the cry of many a hopeful mother. Peter forgot his previous story and now asserted that they were Caspar, Melchior, and Balthazar, the Three Kings of Cologne. Peter was fond of mystification. But the hotel books and the Budlongs gave more authentic accounts. Henceforth patrols of marriageable daughters were about Ira's path; but we shall regard them no more than did he.

De Châteaunéant, swaggering up the hall before dinner, had seen Sir Comeguys. He seemed to recognise and desire to avoid him, and had kept out of the way carefully. Miss Arabella was therefore solitary, as old Bud adhered to his wife, which, perhaps, accounted for the fact that she was not blossoming so luxuriantly as usual.

"Miss Arabella is not a bad girl," remarked Peter Skerrett to Waddy at dinner. "The mother—such a mother!—is ruining her, as she has already spoiled poor Tim. I abhor that woman." Peter was usually very cool and non-committal, but he grew quite excited at this moment. "Look now at her *étalage*," he continued, referring to her low-neck. "What fun it is—a watering-place! I'm so romantic that I have to come here every year for a week to be taken down. I should positively be falling in love with women if I didn't see them here occasionally."

"Why not stay away and be romantic near cottages rose-embowered?" suggested Waddy. "The damsels who trim the roses are fresh as they are pure—what these others are doesn't in the least matter."

"Gammon! Pardon me," said Peter quickly. "That observation was addressed to the waiter—ham, I meant. Can a man like myself seek his love among hollyhocks and marigolds? Really, whatever I may say, I'm not quite spoony enough for female society, except when the band is playing melting strains of passionate despair from some Italian opera, and I am far enough distant therefrom not to observe false notes and brassiness."

"You seem to be sentimental now," said Waddy, smiling. "Who is it? Can it be Miss Arabella? I am interested there, too, in a godfatherly way. I will help you to lynch hot nubbless, as Mr. Budlong calls him. What do you say?"

"No, thanks," said Peter, his cheeks somewhat unnaturally bright. "He'll take himself off when he's won all he can from Tim and the other boys, unless he can marry some of the girls—and then, as Squire Western says, one would hate like the deuce to be hanged for such a rascal. I don't believe Miss Arabella would allow him so much about her, if it were not for her step-mother. I think the infernal blackleg has the mother in his power and she intends to sacrifice the daughter to save herself!" and Peter took a draught of ice-water, against his better judgment, for he was growing quite unnaturally heated.

"Peter! Peter!" protested Waddy, "I'd be afraid your imagination had become perverted by dealing so much with the protective scandals—but I'd come nearly to the same conclusion myself. I saw too much on board the steamer. I said all I could to old Bud."

It was on account of this conversation that Mr. Waddy, seeing Miss Arabella alone after dinner, joined her and chatted a while. Mr. Waddy, though he allows himself to swear in several distant languages, and is altogether perfectly independent in his conduct, will, I hope, already have shown himself a man of refinement in feeling and manner. Women have tact enough to adapt themselves to such men and often humbug them for a time. Miss De Flournoy's altered manner, as she promenaded with Ira, was not humbug, but the unconscious effect of gentlemanly influence.

Long absence from Society, so called, had given Mr. Waddy a large appetite to taste whatever it might have to offer of nutriment or tidbit. He was not a gourmand for scandals, nor a gourmet for gossip. Food is food. Yet grub may not be ambrosia, and, *certes*, nectar is not swipes. On the whole, he remained a-hungered. Ecstasy he was not expecting; he had outgrown such hope by fifteen years. Amusement he found. He had banquets sometimes and sometimes feasts infestive; people dined him for various reasons; he was made rather a lion. Peter Skerrett was inexhaustibly amusing. Under his auspices, Mr. Waddy and his friends came judiciously to know all the delectable people and all the desirables not so delectable. When the autocratic gentlemen at the Nilvedere Hotel expended fifteen dollars in pink buckram for decorations and gave a ball, Ira was invited, of course. When soon after Mr. Belden's arrival, that gentleman, after an unusually successful subscription night, persuaded Mrs. Aquiline to matronise a picnic, Mr. Waddy and his friends were of the party. Mr. Belden gave out publicly that this picnic was for Diana. To Mrs. De Flournoy Budlong he whispered that it was in honour of their acquaintance and rapid intimacy.

Mr. Belden would hardly have been willing that Diana should know how great this intimacy had become. She was not likely to hear the scandals of the Millard; and it is not to be denied that the intimacy soon became one of the most delectable of the said scandals. Julia Wilkes and Milly Center talked it over and knew quite too much about it. Mrs. Aquiline remembered that she was *née* Retroussée, and with a subdued delight kept the rector of St. Gingulphus fully informed. Rev. Theo. Logge, who was by this time well into the Lee Scuppernong, smacked his lips over the flirtation and hoped to Mrs. Grognon that there was nothing wrong.

"A foo paw," he said, "would bring terrible disgrace upon the congregation of St. Aspasia."

And then Logge indited two letters to the *Preserver*. The religious letter bewailed the immorality of the fashionable world, in the pious style of generalisation, and referred to the "dreadful developments in the communication of our secular correspondent, Phylac Terry." Phylac did not develop anything; he confined himself to liquorish innuendos.

Whenever Mrs. Budlong was out with her *étalage* in the parlours, Mr. Belden might have been seen hanging over and inspecting it. There was no hour when they were not together. Belden's bolter came into play for buggy drives at solitary hours, and though he was willing to conceal the qualities of that singed cat, Knockknees, he rode him cautiously by her side on the beach. The sun went down, dimmer grew the horizon where it met the sea, dusk and dim and far-away, falling upon the boundlessness of sea. With the glow and the glory of sunset, gay files of carriages had left the beach, struggled over the stones, and climbed the dusty hill. But Mr. Belden and his companion lingered. She was saying little and sometimes hardly listening, thinking perhaps of girlish escapades on horseback, stampedes upon a bareback pony over meadow or among the pumpkin piles of her father's orchard long ago,—ah! how long it seemed!—when she was simpler and possibly purer than now. Purer? Ah! this seemed a thought she was willing to dismiss, and Drummer suffered for her wish to fly from it. He tore madly on through the dim twilight, she looking back almost fearfully. When that gallop was over, she was again ready to devote herself to her cavalier, letting him bend over the saddle and rearrange her dress.

Peter Skerrett did not like this at all and spoke to Mr. Budlong, who came and went every week. Old Bud told him that since his wife had frankly given up the Frenchman, she should have her own way. He trusted her fully, he said—good soul!

Peter had no right to interfere. Mr. Waddy had no right. No one had. No one ever has. Women and men go on ruining themselves, and the world winks and lets them.

Nor had Peter any right to interfere in Miss Arabella's flirtation with De Châteaunéant. He therefore kept away and the flirtation intensified. Mrs. Budlong patronised it.

Peter could not interfere in Master Tim's subscriptions. Tim was of age, his father's partner. What if he chose to subscribe? Peter used to drop in at the subscription rooms and watch the young rake's progress. The principal subscriptions were in private—it was then that De Châteaunéant made his heaviest collections. He was a most accomplished and successful collector. It may have been that he occasionally allowed Tim to get somewhat in arrears; it was well enough to have Miss Arabella's brother under obligations.

Peter Skerrett inquired of Rev. Logge whether all his tract societies were supplied with agents.

"I could recommend you," says Peter, "a most surprising beggar who gets money out of everyone, as Agent for the Society for Making Tracks."

In fact, to both Peter and Mr. Waddy, the colour of the nobleman's legs became daily more offensive. They were usually clad in violet cassimere, with a flowered stripe, as is the manner of noblemen of his particular rank. But to the two gentlemen they seemed dyed of darkest Stygian hues.

Peter Skerrett, to distract himself from these anxieties, though he denied that he felt any or was concerned for the Budlongs, otherwise than as an amateur of scandals, took Sir Comeguys under his protection. Like a European courier, he would allow no one to cheat that ingenuous youth but himself. Thus there is a Skerretty congruity in the wild legends of American life which luridly light the pages of "Tracks in the Trail of the Bear and the Buffalo." Gyas Cutus and Cloanthus, when they were off duty with Miss Julia Wilkes, were constantly on the watch for Sir Com. They liked to be seen with the baronet, and were ardent to "sell" him, as they called it. But these mercantile transactions, more satisfactory to the seller than to the sold, Peter Skerrett interfered with.

"You'd better take care, Guy, you and old Clo," he said, to the pair of pleasant knaves. "This son of perfidious Albion may be green, but he is plucky and you may get your heads punched. That wouldn't do, because they are soft and the indentures caused by such punching would remain and make it hard to fit you with hats. Abstain and be wise!"

"Do let us have a shy at him, Peter," pleaded Gyas. "His ancestors and mine fought at Bunker Hill—I wish to revenge the death of General Warren."

"Your ancestors?" replied Peter. "Who told you that you ever had any? They may have been tadpoles or worse at that heroic period. Certainly, your grandfather, the first human Gyas Cutus I ever heard of, was only a grade above the tadpole when he kept the Frog Huddle Pond House, near what was then the village of Newark in Jersey. We allow you to associate with us because you're not such a very bad fellow when you're properly bullied; but don't try to come the ancestor dodge—except in that neat and evidently inherited way you have of mixing drinks."

"Well, don't be too hard on a feller," said Guy. "Come and make it seven bells—*tomar las once*, as the Dagoes say—I learned that from a sailor yesterday aboard of Blinders' yacht."

"You're learning to mar all hours with tipple. I shall have to whisper to the fair Julia, unless you swear off," threatened Peter.

"I swear enough, off and on, don't I, Clo? But the tipple tap won't stop. I believe I'll knock off everything but bourbon, as you told me to do before."

"Do," said Peter encouragingly. "The deterioration in our race is completely checked since native wines and bourbon came in. Take plenty of bourbon, and if you ever have a son, possibly he may have a beard. Think of that!"

- 78 -

CHAPTER XV
MR. WADDY RECEIVES A LETTER AND GETS OUT HIS PISTOLS

IT was about this time that Mr. Waddy received the following letter from Mr. Tootler:

"THE SHRINE, August, 1855.

"DEAR IRA:

"I have leased your store, No. 26 Waddy Buildings, to Godfrey Bullion & Co., for five years at $5000 a year.

"Wool is up and fleecing prospers. I am glad, for Mrs. T. asked me the other day what I thought had better be the name of our boy. How would you like to be N. or M. to him—Ira if it's he, Irene if it's a girl? Ira and Irene—Wrath and Peace—that's just the difference between boy and girl.

"But this is not what I am writing about. You know, my dear old boy, that I was never inquisitive about your affairs. Still, you can't suppose that I have not divined something with regard to you and a certain old friend of ours. I don't ask information now, because I believe if you had the right, you would have given it long ago.

"Of course you remember Sally Bishop. The day after you bought Pallid, Cecilia went over to see her. (The dear girl is always going to see people that have diseases. I wonder she don't take the smallpox and yellow fever twice a month the year round.) It seems old Bishop had spoken of you, and when my wife arrived, Sally, who is dying fast, was very curious to hear more. Cecilia was surprised to find that Sally knew you, but would have supposed her inquiries only the ordinary interest of a neighbour in the return of a neighbour, except for something very singular in her manner. Sally asked if you were as fine-looking as ever. Mrs. T., of course, gave the proper reply. Were you married? Did you look happy? Cecilia thought it a strange question—but said that though you were cheerful and very amusing, she found you sometimes very sad—she had observed, in fact, as I had, that there seemed to be some unhappiness at the bottom of your indifferent manner. Sally Bishop burst into tears, in such a distressed and almost agonised manner that my wife feared she would kill herself with weeping. Cecilia prayed her to say what this meant, and she answered in a frightened voice, 'Remorse!'—she would not or could not say anything more, and has always refused to see Cecilia since.

"I have good reason to suppose that Sally had at one time the most intimate relations with Belden. She may have been his mistress. I only much suspect, without being able to fully prove. There was a child, a *filius nullius*, who died, and it was the feeling of shame at this, though I believe that not five people knew it, that drove her father to hard drinking.

"Ira—what cause can she have to feel remorse at the mention of your name? Is it possible that she may have been drawn by Belden into some devilish plot against you? And against someone else?

"I can make no conjectures, as I do not know facts enough. Cecilia, who seems to have her own theory, which she will not impart, will endeavour to learn more from Sally.

"Meantime, do you watch Belden! I know that he went several times to see Sally, and each time she was more ill. He is capable of anything, the rotten villain!—as two of my family know, Cecilia and myself. Is he disposed to be friendly with you now? Something may appear in conversation, if you have a clew. Watch him!

"Yours,

"Thomas Tootler."

Mr. Waddy read this letter very carefully twice. He folded and filed it with a bundle of old yellow letters, written in a hand like his own, with so much difference only as there may be between writing of man and boy-man. He then, with the same extreme deliberation, took from a portmanteau a mahogany box. In it were two eight-inch six-shooters, apparently fired only once or twice for trial. Both were loaded in every barrel of the cylinder with conical ball. The caps were perfectly fresh, but Mr. Waddy changed them all.

While he was thus engaged, Major Granby came in.

"At your armory, eh?" he asked. "You were always a great amateur in shooting-irons. What's in the wind now? You look like an executioner. What do you intend to slay—beast, man, or devil?"

"If I shoot, it will be to slay all three in one," said Waddy gravely.

He had a manner of intense and concentrated wrath, quite terrible to see. The Ira of the man's nature was dominant.

Granby understood that this meant mischief.

"Do you want me?" he asked, quick but quiet.

"Not yet," replied his friend; "perhaps not at all. I don't like to talk of shooting until the time comes to do it. Aiming too long makes the hand tremble. You can understand, Granby, that the world becomes a small and narrow place to walk in when we meet an enemy deadly and damnable. Now, without nourishing any ill-feeling, I begin to half perceive that there may be a person whose life and mine are inconsistent. You said I looked like an executioner—it may be that I shall be appointed executioner of such a person."

"I know you too well," said Granby, "to suppose you capable of any petty revenge—this is grave, of course."

"It is grave. Personal revenge is necessary for the protection of society. There is crime that laws take no notice of. Public opinion—public scorn—is never quite reliable. Nor does public opinion protect the innocent ignorant. There may be such an absolutely dastard villain that, for the safety and decency and habitableness of the globe, he must die—and it is fortunate for society when he outrages anyone to the point of deadly vengeance."

"Do you begin to see any light on the part of your life that we have talked over by so many campfires? Fifteen years is long to wait."

"No years are lost while a man is learning patience. I remember that it took thirty years of my life to teach me to regard my moral and mental tremors and stumbles and falls with the same unconcern that in my fifteenth year I did my childish physical weaknesses. I suppose that one hour of actual happiness now, which I am certainly not likely to have, would explain my dark fifteen years. Patience!"

"You expect to win happiness by killing your man, eh?" questioned Granby.

"No; if I kill him, it will merely be from a quickened sense of duty. Don't think I'm going to lie in ambush like a Thug. I wait information and entertain a purpose."

Here, Sir Comeguys knocked at the door. They had an appointment for a sailing party.

As they passed the parlour, Belden was sitting with Mrs. Budlong. It was as much contact as was possible in public, and some women allow liberal possibilities.

"How much that Belden looks like your friend Dunstan," said Granby. "No compliment to Dunstan, who is just the type American, chivalrous, half-alligator, not without a touch of the non-snapping but tenderly billing and cooing turtle. A graceful union of Valentine and Orson. He is the finest fellow I have seen and his giant friend, Paulding, is made of the same porcelain in bigger mold. They seem to have been everywhere and seen and done everything, except what gentlemen should not do. You'll do well, Ambient, to model after them for your Yankee life."

"Doosed fine fellows," said Ambient, "and Dunstan has told me lots about buffalo hunting. This fellow may look a little like Harwy Dunstan—but he is older, seedier, and hawder. Harwy looks as fresh as Adam before the fall. If he was not such an out-and-outer and my fwiend, I should be savage at him for cutting me out with Diana. She seemed to like him, by George!—fwom the start."

"I thought it was Miss Clara," said Ira, "and that Granby would be gouging the young hero. Paulding seems to me more devoted to Diana."

"Do you know," said Granby, "to pass from bipeds to quadrupeds—that Mr. Belden is trying to make up a race with that wide-travelling horse of his? I heard him phrase it the other day that he could 'wipe out' Pallid."

"If he should offer a bet on that, I wish you would take it—for me, you understand—to any amount," said Ira. "His horse is a singed cat, but Pallid don't need any fire singeing him to make him go. I didn't think he could go as he does, but he is working into it every day."

"Belden won't stand a very large bet. He has been subscribing, as they call it, to the Frenchman lately. Are both those men lovers of your fat friend's wife? What villains some women are! Bless them!" said Granby. "Didn't you tell me, Ambient, that you had seen that Frenchman somewhere?"

"I'm looking at him every day," replied Sir Com. "I lost a thousand pounds to some fellows in Pawis two years ago. I was gween then—a pwecious sight gweener than I am now. Those fellows showed me about Pawis, and all I know of the money is that I lost the thousand one night at what they call a pwivate hell. I was vewy dwunk at the time, I'm ashamed to say, and have no doubt they plucked me. I'm almost suah that this Fwenchman is one of the same chaps. He's diffewently got up, but if I can spot him (as Skewwett says) I shall pound him more or less—more, I think."

"Do so, O six-feet Nemesis! and you will take the house down. If you will mill the Gaul and Waddy beat that contemptible fellow in the race—*Io triumphe!* which means I not only owe but will pay a triumphal supper."

With talk like this, the gentlemen arrived at the wharf. Why the boat they embarked in should be called a "cat," they could not discover. A cat is fond of fish, as the poet hath it——

"What female heart can gold despise?

What cat's averse to fish?"

Newport female hearts of the summer population despise not, but, several of them at least, do fitly esteem the yellow boys, and Newport cats and those who sail in them are not averse to fishing for fish and taking them. So Waddy smiled with his friends and thought too much of Tootler's letter. He would watch Belden.

Meantime, Mr. Waddy saw the world continuously,—and continuously was lionised. This has its pleasures and its pains. It does not build up lofty structures of respect towards the lioniser. Mr. Waddy, however, always had the charm of sweet refuge with his cousin, as he called her, Clara, fairest of the fair, and her friend, the divine Diana. Mrs. Waddy made immense dinner parties for the Returned Kinsman, where he met the people one meets in that best world, of which his hostess is so distinguished an ornament, etc.

The particularly distinguished guest of that summer was the Hon. and Rev. Gorgias Pithwitch, the epideiktic sophist of the nadir Orient. Mr. Pithwitch was sometimes called "The Wizard of the North." He drew immense houses to his pleasant jugglery. He had, that summer, as always, excellent man! some amiable charity to assist—such as to relieve Mahomet's coffin from the painful uncertainties of its position—or to purchase ashes of roses to fill the cenotaph of Mausolus. Anything elegiac or pensively sepulchral gave him a cue for epideiktics or showing off.

Mr. Pithwitch spoke on the character of Mahomet at Newport at the request of the Ladies' Coffin Down Society. All the people who figure in this history went. People always go to hear things. The boys and girls thought the oration "thweet," and so it was—just about. Mr. Belden went with Mrs. Budlong and whispered her safely through, playing meanwhile familiarly with the fringe of her flounces. How they began to eye each other now, those two! Tim Budlong escorted Miss Saccharissa Mellasys. A young poet, Edmund Waller by name, had fallen desperately in love with the soft, startled eyes of Saccharissa. She cast upon him sugar-melting glances, and he loved. Girls like poets and poets like girls. But Edmund, in the intervals of his sonnetteering Miss Mellasys, had been so unfortunate as to beat Tim Budlong regularly at billiards. Tim was in a porcupine state of mind and resolved to be revenged. He devoted himself to Saccharissa and she, well-knowing the cipher of the poet's fortunes and the *chiffre* of Tim's, reciprocated the devotions. They first began to appear together in public at Pithwitch's oration. People began to whisper. It was at this period of his life that Waller wrote his spasmodic poem, "The Beldame, or Blasted Hope."

Mrs. Waddie, as has been said, made a dinner for Mr. Pithwitch. It was part of her active business in society to have all the lions properly treated, and this was not the first whom Mr. Waddy had met at her house. Mr. Pithwitch was, of course, an accomplished, gentlemanly person and very much liked.

"So that is your type orator," Mr. Waddy murmured through his cheroot to Dunstan, as they walked home together; "the best among a myriad talkers from a platform. I suppose he's not able to balance himself on a stump, and therefore is not out doing his duty to what you call the Cause of Freedom in this campaign. Is he ardent for that Cause? Is he ardent for any cause? Is he a strong fiery spirit? I trow not. Tell me of him."

Whereupon Dunstan gave Ira that sketch of the character and genius of Mr. Pithwitch which has just been read. Dunstan was quite familiar with the men of this country who had done aught to distinguish themselves, either positively or negatively. The active life he had led had given him an independence of thought not common among scholars. He had already been through some tough political experience in California in the Free State struggle and was now, on his re-establishment at home, nominated for Congress in his North River district to replace a person who had voted for the Nebraska bill. Dunstan was wanted at this very time in the county of his nomination, and on the stump everywhere; he was a young man of fervid and passionate nature, quite untrammelled by any law of life other than his own sense of right. If he was needed elsewhere, why did he stay at Newport? Men will often stay where they should not, longer than they should, for several reasons, but principally for female ones.

Ira and Dunstan were much together. They talked over society and socialisms at much greater length than can be here repeated. The younger man represented the party of confident hope—the elder did not see life, living, and livers in such brilliant colours. Perhaps his sight was jaundiced.

In fact, for all his friends of the best, and for all his lionising, Mr. Waddy did not cease to be often lonely and often forlorn. Was he growing bilious again, or bored, that he found himself uneasy and unhappy, and became again often filled with bitter longing, and was forced to harden his heart with study of a certain old yellow letter? He knew also that it would be well if he looked less at his pistols. It seemed an unworthy thing to be a spy upon Mr. Belden's movements. He saw that that gentleman avoided him and he indulged himself in interferences with this artful dodger—not spitefully, but because he wished to observe him, and because he did not love that a man he so thoroughly distrusted should have power anywhere with anyone who might confide.

All this was unhappy, unhealthy business. Why return for such life as this? He began to talk with Granby of their journeys and their hunts proposed; but Granby, who, perforce, had become a Stoic, hopeless of any return to his happy happiness, satisfied himself very well where he was. There were snipe and plover to be bagged; the bay still yielded as good fish as had ever been taken. All the ladies who rode were ready to be companioned by so distinguished a cavalier. All who drove thought him an agreeable and decorative object on the front seats of the drivers' drags. He knew all the catsmen of the docks. At every yachting party he, as well as Waddy, was an indispensable. He bathed; he danced; he astonished people at late, sleepy breakfasts by coming in with vast appetite from seven-league walks and presenting this pallid danseuse of the last night's hop with a wild rosebud from a hill a dozen miles away, or that weary, nightless, ballful dowager with a creamy, new-laid egg. He held his own at the club, at billiards with the three ponies of the summer: with Mr. Skibbereen, the cool, cautious man and dashing player: with Blinders, the dashing man and accurate, mathematical player: with Bob O'Link, the sentimental man and nonchalant player. Poor Bob O'Link used to hum lugubrious airs, such as the serenade from "Trovatore," and sigh to Granby, particularly when he made a scratch, that a man whose destiny it was to be a poet could only attain to billiard-marker results.

"I'm too lucky," said Bob O', "to lose money. Then I might grow poor and work. But I'm like Cæsar—wasn't it *Cæsar aut nullus?*—everything I touch turns to gold." And then he would make a lunging stroke that the tyros talked of all summer.

"Poor fellow!" said Granby. "You have reason to be a disappointed man. I've known whole families in the same condition. You'll have to marry a strong-minded woman and learn to run a sewing machine."

"I don't see any strong-minded women," replied Link, looking into an empty chalk-cup for chalk.

"There's Miss Anthrope," suggested Granby. "Besides, Peter Skerrett says it's one of the oldest and most respectable families. They came in, did the Anthropes, with the creation. Marry her."

"Now you mention it, I believe I will," cried Bob; and he did. And Miss Anthrope, now Mrs. O'Link, is one of the lights of the woman's question, while Bob O' is really happy at home in a cradle Elysium, and would not give an obolus to be ferried back to the mundane joys of his former life.

Major Granby was thus, in truth, useful as well as agreeable, and with the feelings of a man who is doing his duty towards himself and incidentally towards others, including his protégé, Ambient, he determined to keep Mr. Waddy at Newport.

I should be doing great injustice to Granby did I fail to say that, with all his pretence of personal enjoyment, it was mainly on Ira's account that he stayed. Granby had not found his friend any less malcontent out of the world than in it. He had seen the same dreariness and utter dissatisfaction overcome him in camps, in desert or forest; under the special and immediate influence of Nature, kindly restorer, he had seen him unrestored. Not that his friend was morbid, inactive, sulky, dull, selfish—never these. Such traits terminate companionship, if not friendly regard. Ira was always, when the time came for exertion, alert, bold, a trapper of the most up-to-trap kind. But when the moment's fleeting purpose was o'ertook, he seemed to care not for changing purpose into result. When need for vivacity ceased, he returned into gloom. His mental hermitage was always ready, where he could become a Trappist of the Carthusian variety. Voyaging over the wild regions of the earth had done him no good. Granby saw that his friend had not been happy out of society. The old wrong, whatever it was, rankled—but it was old. Might it not become out of date, obsolete? No man can ever forget, no man wishes to forget; but he can console himself. Why could not Mr. Waddy love, or like in the range of loving, someone who might be made a wife of? That would distract him—in one or other sense.

"There is the beautiful Clara, his cousin. How happy might a man be in loving her," thought Granby, with a sigh for himself. "That fancy of hers which I have detected for Dunstan, will pass away when she sees he is Diana's. Of course Waddy is charmed with Clara. I believe the dog actually presumes upon his kinsmanship and youthful antiquity to the point of a kiss—confound him!"

CHAPTER XVI
IN WHICH MR. HORACE BELDEN PROSPERS CERTAIN PLANS

DIANA had been left a few days with Miss Sullivan. It was pleasant after the wide, rolling sea, dreary sometimes and lonely in its grandeur, to look quietly across the tranquil lawn upon a cultivated landscape, full of life and homes of seeming happy lives. Summer was ripening all along the gentle slopes—a pleasant, quiet summer for Diana and her hostess, and they spent the few days of Diana's stay in closest confidence.

Mr. Belden did not call upon Diana at Miss Sullivan's, but he discovered the day of her departure. A carefully considered chance made him a passenger on the same train. He did not appear until Miss Sullivan had taken leave of her former pupil. Diana had no fear of travelling alone. Railroad conductors are among the errant knights of modern chivalry; but I never heard that Diana needed protection. She could wither impertinence with a look. But though she did not need an escort, she did not hate one, and when Belden came up with the manner of his better self, she made place and accepted him as companion of dustyish hours.

Diana was happy that day. Her talks with Miss Sullivan had cleared away much darkness from her mind. She was younger by many years than a week before. All the beautiful sights and scenes of her past fleeted before her in bright and changing pictures. She was thinking much of her free and huntress life in Texas. She could even forget the terrible death of her mother. The whole story of that dreadful event was no longer a dark secret with her and one other, and that other she no longer dreaded to meet—that other she need no longer exclude from her presence and her thoughts.

A few hours with Miss Sullivan had changed the current of her life. She was no longer drifting hopelessly toward maddening terrors, forever in dread of herself lest she should yield to a hope that she must deem sacrilege. She had called Miss Sullivan mother, and when that lady, studying her, perhaps by the light of some bitter experience of her own, had said, like a mother firm and wise, "My child! you are hiding something from me," Diana flung herself into this mother's arms, and with such agonised tears as you had not looked for in her clear and fearless eyes, told the secret that had been with her like a death—between her and God and hope and life and love.

And now that this, her mother, had shown her how her guiltless and natural terrors were only superstitions, and how she might blamelessly accept an offered happiness, should it ever offer, there was no more vision of death between Diana and the beloved hopes of her soul.

Yet she did not wish to think of the future; therefore she was glad to be diverted in her journey by an agreeable companion. And to him, also, it was good to be with her. This radiant nature shone upon him, and if there was anywhere in his being a dwarfed and colourless germ of better emotion among the thickets of his daily thoughts, this now sprang up and seemed ready to flourish and blossom. Belden, the petted and successful man, did not with Diana promise himself his usual easy triumph. He was willing to win her by pains. But sometimes in this day, her manner was so transparently full of happiness, and to him was so frank and gracious, that he began to draw inferences rapidly favourable to himself.

You have, perhaps, my young gentleman reader of more or less purity of mind and ardent temperament, sat apart in a poisoned mental ambush watching the woman you loved, while some quite unworthy personage, quite vulpine or quite viperine, was pouring into her ears talk that made you feel like a fox-hound or a snake exterminator. It was not that the talk itself was poison—it was, perhaps, no more than easy clap-trap, shining and shallow, cleverish things, such as may suit a weekly newspaper, philosophy of a man-about-town, gossip from all the courts from the Grand Lama to Brigham Young—the very subjects yourself would, like the cosmopolite you are, have descanted on, were it not that here you could only breathe phrases deep and devoted. It is not the talk that troubles you; it is that the talker, a man you know to be false and foul, should bring his presence so near your shrine of vestal purity. But pardon him, the viper, that he eloquently orates, and pardon her, the Loved One, that she answers gaily. Viper, under that good influence, has perhaps ceased to be venomous; and the Loved One is perhaps gay for remembering those meaning words uttered by you so tenderly before the serpent trailed in and you retired to discontented ambuscade under the fiery shelter of crimson curtains.

Belden, whether he deceived himself or not, was quite willing to think he had made a conquest of Diana. He was one of those who have been encouraged by vulgarish women, tending toward demirepdom, to think that, when he entered, "all fair, all rich—all won, all conquered stand." Diana was guiltless of any willing coquetry. She was thinking of herself and did not concern herself as to what impression she made upon others. But unwittingly, by the gift of nature, she had all those slight fascinations and winning charms that self-made coquettes study for in laborious hours, and persuade themselves they have attained.

Mr. Belden was, no doubt, properly solicitous for Diana's baggage. This goddess was mundane enough to have made purchases beyond belief of Parisian dresses. "I dare do all that may become a man," but to enter her boxes and describe their contents I dare not. Thinking of Diana, one thought not of the robes, but of the Mistress of the Robes. Belden was experienced in the small cares of society. It was part of his profession as a ladies' man to recognise all properties of his escorted. She therefore arrived unimpaired at Newport. Clara Waddie, who met her at the boat, would hardly have given the escort so cordial a reception. Mr. Belden, probably, did not resemble any friend of hers.

Diana's presence completed the charm of the Waddies' house at Newport, and the house was a worthy temple for its two deities, for Clara had always been the mistress of its decorations, and her cultivation and intuitive judgment were everywhere apparent.

Clara and Diana! the A and B of this C, D, were Dunstan and Paulding, a pair of the best men. A noble thing is the friendship of two brothers in love. California began just as they left college together. They dashed off immediately. Being fellows who were up to anything, they got on wonderfully. They mined, drove coaches, were judges or counsel at the plentiful hangings of the day. Each of them shot a pillager or two and rescued a few Mexicans and Chinamen from pillage by escaped Australians. In the starvation winter, they headed the party that relieved the involuntary cannibals of the Sierra Nevada. They bought a ranch, and finding on its edge among the hills a ready-money boulder of gold, quite an Ajax cast in fact, they opened dry diggings there and took out neat piles before the outsiders came in. Then they took a little run to San Francisco. Everyone who has had California—and what one brave and bold of those days is there that could have it and did not?—every Californian of the early times knows what two men drawing together, not indulging in hebdomadal big drunks or diurnal little drunks, and not beguiled in any sense by the sirens of the Bella Union or other halls, what such a whole team could achieve. These two friends, living together, acting together, having common purse, common purposes for the future, when they had seen the lights and shadows of this phase of life, had gained each the other's good qualities. When they were together in presence, you saw their marked difference of nature, marked as their differences of physique. When they were apart, each seemed the other's counterpart. One sometimes sees this singular likeness in man and wife of some marriage of happy augury.

At San Francisco, they chanced to pick up one of the Mexicans whom they had protected and befriended in the mines. Through him they became interested in a land claim, which the poor fellow had by inheritance. They carried it on in his behalf, and when he died they found themselves by his will owners of the claim. It was made good. They were selling it at the fabulous prices of that day when Paulding was recalled by his mother's death. Dunstan remained to close the business. He was able to remit to his friend wealth for them both.

Dunstan returned home across the plains by New Mexico and Texas. In the up-country of Texas, he was detained some time by an accident. After some delay, he joined his friend in New York. Several years of toil and danger entitled them to brief repose. When action again became necessary to them, they essayed to revive at home the interest they had felt in constructive politics in California, but the ripeness of times had not yet come. The line was not yet drawn upon the great national question of America, which has since made the position of man and man inevitable according to character and education. Politics were not interesting.

Paulding observed his friend falling into melancholy. Since the trip across the plains and the accident in Texas, Dunstan had lost that ardent vigour and careless hopefulness which had made him the leader in their California adventures. Perhaps he had achieved success too early and was blasé. Paulding took his friend to Europe, where they remained knocking about and occasionally amusing themselves with making the aborigines stare with some stupendous California extravagance, until they heard of Frémont's nomination. They knew the man. They had shared with him, and others good and true, the labours of constituting the State of California. He was one after their own hearts—a gentleman pioneer—a scholar forester—a man of untrammelled vigour and truth of character—a Californian, which is a type of man alike incomprehensible to the salon and the saloon. It was the man they wanted; it was also the cause they wanted. They made for home as friends, Californians, and lovers of right, to take part in the campaign. Dunstan was nominated for Congress at home, up the North River. They went to Newport for days a few—they were staying for many days.

Why?

Paulding and Dunstan had known the Waddies and Clara in Europe. The two friends were presented to Diana.

It was all over with Paulding at once—over head and ears. So it happened with too many men who met Diana.

Diana was very happy in these few weeks, brilliantly happy. All their friends came constantly to the Waddies'. At Newport, everyone is at leisure; pleasure is the object. Where it dwells, all go. So the young ladies held perpetual levées without tête-à-têtes.

At these levées Mr. Belden appeared frequently. He was in most amicable and laudatory mood. He pleased both the ladies by speaking in terms almost affectionate of Miss Sullivan. He had known her, he said, from his boyhood. They had been playmates in the fresh days of childhood. Many a morning he had gone proud to school with her rosebud in his buttonhole. They had grown up together, like brother and sister—no, more like cousins. He spoke of it with some sentiment. She was very lovely then.

"She seems to me still very lovely," said Diana. "The loveliest woman I have ever seen. There is a serene sweetness and tranquillity in her beauty. No one else has that look of tender resignation. She is my idea of Faith."

Belden uttered a strange sound like a sigh.

"Yes," he said, "she is what you describe. She has had need of resignation after so much domestic trouble—her father's disgrace—their poverty. And then her life of teaching—ah! that can hardly have been miserable, with pupils like you, young ladies! We can hardly regret that she was compelled temporarily to leave her own sphere for the purpose of educating you to fill yours so charmingly."

"You are flattering Miss Sullivan through us," retorted Diana. "We thank you in her name. You cannot praise her too highly. She is wise and good and noble. Only I could wish that she were not so sad."

"Let us hope that her spirits will improve, now that she is rich in the means to do good," Belden said.

In the same laudatory strain he spoke of Mr. Waddy.

"He, also, was one of my playmates. We have been separated for several years, but I hope to revive our old intimacy here."

"Was he always the same odd, hasty, irascible, placable person?" asked Clara.

"Yes," replied Belden; "we called him at school Ira the Irate. It was always a tropical climate wherever he was. I do not wonder he found our boreal Boston too chilly for his nature."

"He does not resemble at all the typical nabob," observed Diana. "He is not fat and curry-coloured. He does not wear yellow slippers and Madras cravats and queer white clothes of the last cycle. He sits a morning with us and does not ask for ale. He doesn't call lunch tiffin. In fact, if he did not have a Chinese servant and smoke an immense number of cheroots, one could scarcely observe anything in which he differs from other men of the world."

"How much Chin Chin looks like Julia Wilkes's friends, Mr. Cutus and Mr. Fortisque," said Clara.

"Those two unfortunate youths, with chop-stick legs, no perceptible moustache, complexions *de foie gras?*" and Belden laughed. "The bohoys call them Shanghais. They are indeed changeling Chinese—not quite men. There is in South America one variety of monkey that has a moustache—most have not—they have not."

"Why does Julia allow such amorphous objects to be perpetually before her?" asked Diana.

"They have surrounded her," Clara replied. "She is very good-natured and not very wise. One of them is always standing sentinel. I suppose no clever man likes to have a sprightly fool forever standing by and filling vacancy with smiling dumminess while he is talking. So the clever men have actually been thrust away from poor Julia by these two pertinacious friends."

"Very different from your two civilised California friends," said Belden, still in a complimentary vein.

"Did you know them in California?" asked Diana.

"No; I was in San Francisco. They were up the country. They were well known from their efficiency in relieving the starved emigration of '49, and from the very active part they took [G— d—n them!] in making California a free State."

Belden went on commending judiciously the friends, whom he hated on general principles and found in his way at present. He relieved himself by internal salvos of cursing and achieved his object of buttering all his antagonists, so that he could slip by, as he hoped, and win the prize. He *must* win. Yes. Or what?

"How handsomely he spoke of Paulding and Dunstan," said Clara, after he had gone. "I must learn to think better of a man who has the rare virtue of not being jealous."

"Can it be," said Diana, "that he was ever attached to Miss Sullivan? He speaks almost tenderly of her. I have noticed a certain coolness or awkwardness between them hardly to be accounted for in any other way. If it is so, he shows another rare trait, that of remembering without unkindness a woman who has rejected him."

So this serpent charmed away Clara's prejudices, or for a moment persuaded her that she was unjust, and beguiled Diana into something more like intimacy. They, as innocent women, knew very little of the man. And, indeed, there were no positive charges against him, except that he was what is pleasantly called a "lady-killer." Their gentlemen friends, though sharing in the general distrust of him, had no brother's privilege of warning against an acquaintance, if merely undesirable. Therefore, the ladies did not hear of Mr. Belden's flirtation with Mrs. Budlong. The Waddies did not know her. Her storming of good society had taken place during their absence. Mr. Belden, in reply to their inquiries, spoke of her with respect.

Diana, at this time, occasionally felt a slight recurrence of that pain in her side which has already been noticed. Once when Belden was accompanying her in a ride, a privilege he now frequently had, this pain for a moment overcame her terribly. She would have fallen but for his ready aid and judgment. She was restored in a moment and insisted upon continuing her ride. Belden was even better received than usual when he called in the evening to make proper inquiries. He had shown a very respectful delicacy and was rewarded by gratitude and an invitation to dinner. He congratulated himself upon his luck and hoped the lady would faint every day.

Diana was seized with this same pain one evening when she was sitting a little apart with Dunstan. He sprang to support her. She had strength to repel him, almost rudely. Clara retired with her a moment till the spasm passed. When the gentlemen took their leave, which they did immediately upon the ladies' re-entrance, Diana gave her hand to Dunstan, as if to apologise. Her manner was grave, even solemn, as she said to him some commonplaces of thanks for his intended courtesy.

Clara felt some anxiety for her sister-friend. What meant these sudden pains? Diana made light of them. They were nothing, transitory only—a reminder of an unimportant hurt she had received in Texas. She was perfectly well—and so she seemed, brilliantly full of life, that must sing and laugh and blush at each emotion.

There arose a singular coolness between the sisters at this time—a lover's quarrel, as it were; and yet no quarrel, but a seeming hesitancy before some more perfect confidence. They were more affectionate than ever when together, but more apart, shunning each other, talking of trifles. Clara was conscious of this partial estrangement. In fact, it was almost wholly on her side. The high and careless spirits of her friend seemed to jar upon her. She seemed to long for solitude. Anywhere but at Newport in the summer, she might have indulged in lonely walks. There she was compelled to encounter the world and be gay with it.

But she grew pale—they told her so. She said it was moonshine. And so it was—beautiful moonshine—sweet, melancholy pallor; but bloom was better. Sorrow, unmerited, came to her—sorrow such as even to herself she could not confess. The wish, the hope that she would not admit, for all its besetting sieges, would make her untrue to herself and disloyal to her friend. Disloyal to Diana—her rival! The first was as far from her thoughts as the last seemed unimaginable. No one could be the rival of Diana!

CHAPTER XVII
MR. BELDEN CONTEMPLATES VILLAINIES,
NEW AND OLD

BELDEN was the only guest at the dinner at Mr. Waddie's in recognition of his care of Diana. It was a satisfactory affair to him, the principal actor. The to eat was good; the to drink sparkling; the to wit brilliant; the to woo he thought promising.

It was not late when Mr. Belden reached the Millard on return from this fortunate occasion. They were hopping, reciprocating to the Nilvederes. There was tempting wealth of *étalage*, but Belden slipped through the side door and up to his room. He took from one of his double-locked trunks a small tin case, such as men who have securities keep them in. He unlocked the case and took from it a bundle of papers, old papers carefully enveloped. They were endorsed "Ira Waddy's Letters."

Belden opened the parcel and looked at several of the letters. Some were signed "Ira Waddy," or "Ira"; some "Sally Bishop." They were such letters as some women exchange with some men, but such as only vile men and women write. Belden seemed to enjoy the tone of these epistles hugely.

"What a bitch that girl was," he said to himself. "Waddy missed it when he was such a Puritan with her. She was a bad one to have for enemy. She thought getting up the letters a glorious joke. How we roared over some passages. I think I should have let the thing drop after proposing it, if she hadn't been so mad for it. It was a devilish risky thing to do. The fellow would kill me in a minute if he knew it, but Sally won't peach before she dies, I think. The other woman is safe, damn her! She and Waddy are the only two people that ever baffled me. But I've had what I call a neat revenge—I should think so. She might much better have smiled upon me for her own good. As to Waddy, he don't seem over-civil now. I shouldn't mind closing the whole thing up by shooting him. Miss Diana seems to have a liking for fighting men. I'm getting on fast with her. She's a little of a bolter, but I can soon tame her, once in hand. Well, I thought I would burn these letters, but they're a little too rich. When I'm engaged to her, I'll burn 'em and reform. Some people would call it forgery—writing those documents—bah! what's forgery!"

He began scribbling names in various hands: his own, Ira Waddy, Diana, Betty Bud, Bet Budlong, Sally Bishop, Tootler, Janeway, Sullivan, Perkins, and others, just as recollection seemed to associate those whom he had known in former life or now.

While he was scribbling, there came a knock at the door.

"Who's there?" called Belden, tossing the papers into their case.

"Hit's me, sir," answered a cockney voice.

Belden unlocked the door and admitted a very bandy-legged groom, neatly enough dressed, but topped by a most knavish head and face.

"Well, Figgins," said his master, "what do you want?"

"Will ye 'ave Knockknees, sir, hin the mornink harely? Ye can go hon the beach hat sevenk."

"Bring him up at seven, then; the race must come off now in a few days. I'm ringing in these precious greenhorns. They'll all run their damned cows, but they haven't got enough to bleed much. I want to get that fellow in with his black horse. He'll bleed gold. Can I beat him on the square, do you think?"

"Hi dunno, sir," said Figgins, "'e's a stepper, his that black. Hi never see such a 'oss for clean goin'. You mout beat, hand you moutn't. But p'r'aps 'e'll be summat sick,—a little sick, 'nough to take the edge hoff 'im hat the race."

"Perhaps he will," agreed Belden, instantly accepting the hint. "You might look at him once or twice and let me know whether it's likely. You know where his stable is—can you get in?"

"There's keys to be 'ad, I s'pose. Do you want 'im to show hat all?"

"Oh, yes, I hope he'll be well enough to make good play. He might win a heat—then I can get more out of 'em. You understand? It will pay you devilish well if I win a jolly pile."

"Hi see, sir," said Figgins, and with a furtive look at the tin case, he went out.

Belden locked the case and put it away. The full luxurious sound of music from the hall swelled up again after a pause and filled the room. Some men are purified from baser wishes by the delicate sensualities of passionate music; but not such men as Belden.

"Ah, a galop!" he thought. "I must go down and have a stampede and hug with Mrs. Bud. Dear Betty Bud! I think I get on rather faster with her than with Miss Diana."

He went to the glass to arrange his toilet for the deranging struggles of the hop. He did not perceive that the look of his three villainies of the evening was stamped upon his face—three, one remembered, two meditated. He thought it was the effect of age, the change he began to be conscious of in his appearance. But age, of those whose lives are worthy to endure, softens and tranquillises expression and harmonises colouring; it does not darken the shadows where they had grown dark on his face, nor give the unpeaceful and uneasy look he had.

"I must hold up for a while," he thought. "I wish I could keep away from that damned faro place. My luck is dished lately. However, I'll make that race square the accounts. If it don't, I'm up a tree."

He went down Jacob's Ladder. Millard's parlour was nearly as deserted as its namesake of political supporters. All the Millarders and the Nilvederes, with a decimation of outsiders and farthermores, were taking their constitutional perspiration bath in the dining rooms—tables having been turned out for the occasion. Trotting polkas, racking redowas, cantering waltzes, galloping galops—bipeds were being put through all their paces.

The old flirtations were going on swimmingly in the damp intervals of dance; and lo! a new one. Bob O'Link was for the first time devoted to Miss Anthrope. That strong-minded young person had, in the most feeble-minded manner, succumbed at once when Bob O' suddenly and newly appeared in the ballroom and unanimously singled her out for a permanent partner.

"Miss Anthrope has decided to take a false position," said Peter Skerrett to Gyas and Cloanthus, who were swabbing and drying off at the door.

"No! Has she, though!" said Gyas. "What is it? She looks to me as well on her pins as usual."

"She is going to marry for money—that is the false position, a pillory that neither man nor woman ever escaped from. Well, Bob O' will stand by her better than most fellows. Look at the chap. He is as sure to win in love, particularly the bought variety, as at billiards."

"Stand by, Peter," said Gyas; "I'm going to say a good thing. Miss Anthrope will be linked to Link, in the links of high man's chain. Capital, isn't it? Now, Clo, don't you get ahead of me and say that to Julia."

"Honour among friends," returned Cloanthus. "I'll take you odds, Guy, on Bob O'Link. Ten to one he gets her in ten days; five to one in five days; two to one on to-morrow—and even it's done to-night."

"You'd better save your money, boys," said Peter. "Not that you'll spend it in charity, but you'll want it all to pay what you'll lose on the race Belden is getting up."

"There he comes now with Mrs. Budlong," said Gyas Cutus. "By Golly, isn't she a stunner! Belden looks deuced hard to-night."

"You'll find him hard enough—hard as one of Millard's eggs. I recommend you both to keep away from him and his horse," said Peter.

Here the music struck up a galop and the two flexible youths, pocketing their moist *batistes*, tore wildly into the affray. Mr. Belden dashed by with Mrs. Budlong in his arms.

He had found her tête-à-tête with De Châteaunéant. Their whispered conversation closed as Belden approached, and bowed his request for a dance. "Hot nubbless" looked after her wickedly as she moved away.

Sir Comeguys, passing with Granby, looked into the parlour. Sir Com saw the Frenchman standing there with his vicious look and his clenched fist.

"Gwanby," said the bold and battailous Briton, "I can't be wong—that is the scoundwel that helped to wob me in Pawis. He called himself Lavallette then, or some such name."

CHAPTER XVIII
THE BRAVE PREPARE FOR A RACE, THE FAIR FOR A PICNIC

NEXT morning after Millard's hop, several of our acquaintance met on the piazza.

"What happened at the subscription party last night?" asked Peter Skerrett of Gyas, who looked blue and slumbrous as a night policeman.

"They didn't do a very heavy business," responded Guy. "Lob Lolly subscribed three hundred. Hobble de Hoy collected two-fifty. Belden lost like leaking. De Châteaunéant was collecting pretty well, till Sir Com Ambient came in and sat down opposite; then he seemed to get flustrated, subscribed once or twice, and went away."

"What an astonishing feller that Belden is!" said Cloanthus. "There he comes in on Knockknees, and we've only just grubbed."

Belden gave his horse to Figgins and lounged up the steps. He affected a dignified indifference with the younger men generally, but this morning he was quite gracious. They were discussing the preliminaries of the race. They had talked of a steeple-chase, but the riders did not come forward very freely, and they had determined to have a formal race; mile heats on the second beach, best two in three, free to all ages, no handicap—in short, a kind of scrub race.

While they were talking it over, Chin Chin brought up Pallid. Mr. Waddy was going for a morning ride with Clara and Diana. There were divers opinions on Pallid's merits. Some of them said he was too handsome to make time— "a good un to go should always be a bad un to look at," and there were instances enough on this side. There were also abundant instances on the other. In short, no one had seen him put to his speed, and none could do more than conjecture how low he would go down in the seconds. A very few seconds make the great differences in horses, as the minor, imperceptible charms distinguish between the few beautiful and the many pretty among women. It was conceded that it was a sin to race on the beach. "The horses' feet will be ruined; the beach is as hard as Macadam." But they had determined to do it. There was an *éclat* about the beach that no other place could have.

Belden said that Pallid was a very fine animal—the handsomest horse he knew—very fast, too; very fast. He was surprised that Mr. Waddy had not entered him. Perhaps Mr. Waddy did not want to win their money—very likely! He couldn't know, of course, anything about the comparative powers of the two horses, but if Pallid were in the race, he wouldn't fear to back his horse against him for a thousand.

"Do you mean that for an offer?" asked Major Granby, joining the group.

"I would make it one if the horse were in the race," answered Belden.

"This is getting interesting," said Peter Skerrett; "and just in time here comes Dunstan, and Mr. Waddy to speak for himself."

The boys crowded round Mr. Waddy to persuade him to enter his horse. Guy and Clo wished to see Belden beat; he had scoffed at them for being imberb.

"Of course," said Mr. Waddy, "anything to please the children; but I can't ride him myself. I carry too much weight for a race. Pallid's only five. I say, Dunstan, don't you want to ride him? You are just my height—five feet ten—but then I outweigh you fifteen pounds—two pounds a year for the difference in our ages."

"I shall be delighted," said Dunstan, "if you'll trust me. Is there anything on it besides the stakes?"

"That is as Mr. Belden pleases," said Granby. "Do you hold to the offer?"

"Certainly," responded Belden, and the bet was booked.

"If I were betting with Belden," said Gyas, aside to Peter Skerrett, "I should want stakes up."

"You would behave with your usual asinine indecorum, Guy, my boy, if you hinted such a thing. Belden is not a man to back down. He'd rather murder somebody and get the money. If he loses, he'll pay. But he don't intend to lose. He knows his horse, and I'd advise you not to bet against him. In fact, the best thing you and Clo can do is to stop betting entirely and put your money in your old boots. I've been talking like a father to you two for years, and you don't improve."

"Why, what do you want us to do, Peter?" asked they penitently, by Gyas, principal spokesman. "Everybody is down on us. We try to do the fair thing. We pay our tailor's bills and don't smoke over five cigars a day. We don't know what to do. Miss Sullivan, up at The Island this summer, used to pitch into us and say we ought to have ambition. Well, I did try politics once and went to the polls to vote. There was an Irish beggar who swore he'd seen me vote twice before. That rather knocked my politics. I've read all Thackeray, and Buck on the 'Sublime,' and Tennyson's 'Sacred Memories,' and the 'Pickwick Club.' Then about religion—I'll be blowed if I can keep awake in church. It's no go. I try every Sunday. The Doctor can't do it, and he's allowed to be the best preacher in the world. I get asleep and have bustin' nightmares on account of the painted windows."

"Well, try to be good boys. Don't bet, and I'll see if I can think of something for you," said Peter.

The season was drawing to a close. There had been no earthquakes of excitement, no avalanches of clean or dirty scandal. Indeed, since the Pithwitch oration, there had been no event at Newport. People actually began to talk of going away too soon. The race, then, was the right thing at the right time. People began to talk of it astonishingly. Major Granby had, people said, ten thousand dollars bet with Mr. Belden. Major Granby was, so report alleged, a younger son of the Marquis of Grimilkin, and had made an enormous fortune on the turf. Rev. Theo. Logge said that he disapproved very much of betting, but that he should ask the winner to contribute to the Cause—he did not say whether the Lee Scuppernong cause or not. He hoped that his sister in the faith, Mrs. Grognon, would not interrupt her drive to the beach for these carnal excitements. Perhaps it was as well that she should see the race, to know for the future what to avoid. He would escort her and gain experience, which would be valuable to him in warning young men not to go to such scenes of temptation.

All the ladies became partisans. Miss Milly Center asked Mr. Dulger if he should ride.

"I've no horse," said Billy, safe in that negation.

"But," said Miss Millicent, "Sir Com Ambient has none, and he says he intends to hire one just for the fun of the start."

Unhappy Billy Dulger, whom nature did not shape to fit a saddle, must not be outdone by Sir Com, whom Milly quoted constantly. Billy consulted a livery-stable man. This personage provided Billy with a four-legged quadruped.

"He won't win the first heat," said the man, "nor perhaps the second; but git him through those, and I shouldn't be surprised at anything."

Bob O'Link entered his horse. Miss Anthrope, her nature seemingly changed with her proximate change of name, hung about him tenderly, praying him not to ride. She preferred that he should not be killed, for with his death would die Mrs. O'Link *in posse*.

Blinders entered a headlong steed. He generally rode him with two snaffles, one around his waist, the other in his two hands. Blinders did not talk about his horse. He was a fellow who always went slap at anything without a word; but he looked at all the horses and thought his own chance was good. His horse was called Nosegay, on account of the gayness of his nose.

Little Skibbereen besieged his mamma to let him enter with Gossoon, but mamma had prejudices against the breaking of Skibby's neck. Scalper, the artist, arrived in time. He would ride Gossoon, who was one of the favourites. Unfortunately, Scalper was too amusing a fellow not to be fat, and he outweighted Gossoon.

Guy and Clo, though *fortes ambo* in a buggy, were not accustomed to bestride the prancing steed. Paulding reserved himself to drive Diana and Clara.

There was question between Tim Budlong and De Châteaunéant which should bounce upon Drummer. When the Gaul discovered that Sir Comeguys was to contend, he remembered that Drummer seemed to have unreasonable prejudices against him, and if he should endeavour to subdue that very priceless steed with spiteful whip and spur, some displeasure might arise on the part of Mr. Budlong. Tim therefore proposed himself and Drummer for victory, and the fair Saccharissa Mellasys bestowed upon him a lovely jockey cap of blue and white satin gores. Tim's face was by this time pale and flabby, and he did not look the handsomer for his fresh head-piece.

Thus, a field of eight was entered, as many as could conveniently start on the beach. Peter Skerrett, by common consent, became the *impresario* of the occasion. Interest rather centred upon Pallid and Knockknees on account of the bet pending. Some of the knowing ones backed Blinders and Nosegay for the purse. A few trusted to Bob O'Link's personal reputation for luck, and one or two backed Drummer, thinking Tim could not possibly persuade him to be beaten.

While the gentlemen were thus ardently preparing for their Olympic games, the ladies also had their scheme of festivity.

"What shall we do for Milly Center on her birthday?" asked Mrs. Wilkes, that unwearied chaperon.

Miss Millicent was not too old to have a birthday on the day before the race. Mr. Dulger was aware of this epoch and had written to Bridgeman for a barrel of flowers. Dulger's clerkly salary—for his stern papa kept him on a salary much too exiguous for his exigencies—his salary hardly sufficed for his systematic floral tributes. He had been obliged to write to the bookkeeper in Front Street for another temporary loan. Billy had presentiments that the crisis of his fate was at hand. He would not fail at the last for want of sufficient investment. A flower barrel was a *grandiose* gift. He was confident that no one else had thought of it. True love makes a Dulger a genius. If the wooed could not be won by a barrel of flowers, he would forever fly her false toleration and among the flour barrels toilsomely regain his wasted bouquet money. Poor Billy Dulger! So long a Tolerated, he was weary of this "longing much, hoping little, asking naught."

"How shall Milly's birthday be honoured?" was, however, still a question for the generality. Each suggested other things and a picnic.

"A picnic, of course," said the masterly Mrs. Wilkes.

"To the Dumplings, of course."

"Yes, of course."

"Why, yes; how could we think of anything else?"

"With a band," said Julia, "and dancing on the grass."

"With a boatload of champagne," said Cloanthus.

"No flirtations allowed," suggested Peter Skerrett.

"No? Well, then, flirtations compulsory; first, with Miss Milly, Queen of the Day, afterwards with our private Queens of Hearts," and he chanted,

"The Queen of Hearts she brought some Tarts

Unto a Picnic gay;

The King of Hearts he ate the Tarts

And gave his Heart away."

It is not very important, but be it hereby known unto thee, O outsider of Kenosha, Stamboul, Fond du Lac, Paris, Natchez under the Hill, London, Lecompton, or Jerusalem! that the Dumplings of Newport *is* an old stone fort, not *are* certain apples enclosed in certain unwholesome strata of dough.

Picnics go to the Dumplings as a shad to fresh water in spring, as a moth to a candle, as a swain to a nymph. They go there in boats over the smooth bay, across the strait, where a soft, lulling prolongation of the distant ocean swell reaches the navigator with sweet reminder motion. When picnics arrive at the Dumplings, they stroll about; their better halves are handed over the rocks by their worse halves; they view that crumbling, cheese-shaped object, the fort, and say sweet things of salt water and sunshine. They chat. They romp. Then comes the climax—to eat the picnic. Picnics are properly eaten with the fingers. The idea is to return to Arcadian manners.

Picnics being well known by all the fair and brave, who deserve each other, as so charming and offering such charming opportunities for attaining their deserts, there is no wonder that everyone was delighted with Mrs. Wilkes's scheme. Miss Millicent, as the heroine of the occasion, gave deep thought to her toilet. She was resolved to be captivating as Miss Millicent, that is for herself; not as Miss Center, that is for her fortune. She had always adorers enough, besides the inevitable Dulger, but he was her thrall and the others she had flirted through. She had been observed to be dissatisfied of late. Was it that she had failed with Sir Comeguys? Or did some other novelty refuse to enter her toils? Or was there some escaped one whom she wished to beguile back again with penitential wiles? Or was she a little ashamed of her exacting, not immoral, *cicisbeism* with poor Billy? For whatever reason, Miss Milly seemed a little disappointed, and Mrs. Wilkes, not thinking it proper that any of her protégées should be out of spirits, hoped well of the picnic, that it would restore the heiress to amiability. So Mrs. Wilkes shopped extravagantly with Miss Milly and the girls.

Clara and Diana were of course to be of the party. They were really the belles. The men who fell in love with Diana that summer, and some of them were stanch old belle-ringers, say that she was the culmination; that there never was and never will be another like her. And then, some stanchest old member of the pack gives tongue and says "Except Clara," and the whole pack cry "Except Clara"—Clara not second in order, but only subsequent in thought.

Everybody, in a word, was to be at the picnic. Everybody means thirty or forty people. Good Mrs. Wilkes had a moment's hesitation about Mrs. Budlong, and privately consulted Peter Skerrett, her Grand Vizier. Peter, with his usual thoughtfulness, pointed out that Miss Arabella couldn't go without her mother; so Mrs. B. was invited. Mrs. Aquiline, *née* Retroussée, had recently begun a dead set at Mr. Waddy. She engaged ardently in the project. There would be a band and a boatload of champagne and a sail home by moonlight.

In short, Miss Milly Center's birthday picnic was to be the event of the season. Her spirits rose as she beheld her most becoming dress, and she prognosticated for herself no solemn epoch of repentance and reform, but an auroral dawn of new flirtations with full recovery of all the old, an *annus mirabilis* of social success and scores of manly hearts trampled under foot.

CHAPTER XIX
MISS CENTER'S BIRTHDAY PARTY AND WHAT OCCURRED THEREAT

THE fateful day dawned. Fair were the omens of the morning; full their accomplishment as day culminated. Oh, what a parade there was! Chiefly and Chieftainly the Millard sent forth its fleet full of younkers and prodigals and "skarfed barks," flaggy with dizzy floating of ribbons. Commodore Mrs. Wilkes headed this centre of the squadron. Commodore? I will rather say Admiral of all the grades, red, white, and blue; *liberté, égalité, fraternité*—these, under her admiral conduct, were to be the watchwords of the day. And now from many a cottage of gentility, from many a sham château, if possible more genteel, they were pouring and thronging in full-sailed bravery toward the rendezvous.

They were landed in a lovely cove near the Dumplings. Mr. Dulger was ardent in his endeavours to aid the Queen of the Day, Miss Millicent, in disembarking; so ardent that Nemesis thought he needed quenching, and so quenched him a little. He slipped knee-deep into the water with a ducking splash. Dunstan handed the lady out, while Peter Skerrett picked Billy up with a mild reproof.

The party was one of many elements; these soon grouped or paired in elemental concord, and all the slopes were gay with the sight of lolly circles, and jocund with the sound of their lively laughter. The band piped unto them and somewhat they essayed to dance upon the undulating sward. It was remarked by the Millarders that Mr. Belden and Mrs. Budlong were absent a long time, and that afterwards he was very devoted to Diana. It was also remarked that Miss Arabella was getting tired of the Frenchman. Dear me! how people do remark things.

Mr. Waddy did not feel out of place at the picnic, because, as a man of the universal world, he was always in place; but he was out of spirits. Tootler wrote no more. Ira was wretched with suspenses and suspicions. Poor old Budlong—here was this wife of his hardly concealing her intrigue with Belden—her second intrigue, and this time not with a blackleg, but with one whom, he feared, was a villain. Belden, too, was intimate with Diana, favoured by Clara; and Ira could not warn them. He had nothing except suspicion. His judgment, sharpened by this, saw Belden as he was—plausible, flattering, laborious to please, cautious of offence, clever, experienced, a man of that very dangerous class who see the better and follow the worse. Mr. Waddy, therefore, seeing Belden's success, was filled with wrath. The old man Ira began to take control of his lately stoical nature.

"I'm getting dangerous," he felt; and not all the petting of Mrs. Aquiline, nor all the attentions of the daughtery mothers and nubile daughters, could distract him or make him distracted from this ugly presence of hateful thoughts. He observed that Belden was uneasy when he was by, and concealed his unease by a seeming cordiality. Mr. Waddy began to tingle with a nervous sensation of presentiment that there was to be a crisis, an explanation, a punishment, a vengeance—what and for what he could not yet foresee.

By-and-by, the happy moment arrived for which all other deeds at a picnic are only preparatory. The edible and potable picnic was announced as ready to be eaten and drunk, and a truly Apician banquet it was—thanks to Mrs. Wilkes, experienced giver of dinners and liberal feeder of mankind. Some of the banqueting was very pretty to behold. Fair ladies are not ignoble in the act of taking ladylike provender. But it must also be allowed that some of the banqueting was not so pretty.

"Look at Rev. Theo. Logge," said Peter Skerrett to Ambient; "he pretends to wish that

"'All the world

Should in a pet of temperance feed on pulse,

Drink the clear stream——'

"But observe, that is not pulse he eats, but pâté of Strasburg, and what he is pouring down is a stream, to be sure, a large one and clear, but it comes from a very poptious bottle. I cannot think it water."

"I say, Peter," says Guy, "let's fuddle the Rev."

"Guyas Cutus," reproved Peter gravely, "you are a pagan. I have frequently remarked that difference between Cloanthus and you. You are a pagan and swear 'I Gaads.' He is a monotheist and swears 'I Gaad'. In this case you can spare yourself a sacrilege. Mr. Logge is fuddling himself. Hillo," he added, looking up suddenly as a cork struck him hard on the ear.

De Châteaunéant had opened a champagne bottle carelessly and had not only bombarded Peter, but had deluged Sir Comeguys. Sir Com looked quietly at the Frenchman, waiting for an apology; none came, but the bottle-holder gave a blackguard laugh. He must have been a little elated by drinking, and reckless. Miss Arabella had been particularly cool to him all day, and it had taken much wine to counterbalance his chagrin. No one saw the little scene except Blinders and Mrs. Budlong, and the banquet went on and off brilliantly.

While the gentlemen were lighting cigars and separating for a few moments from the ladies, Blinders tapped De Châteaunéant on the shoulder.

"Sir Com Ambient would like to say a word to you behind the hill yonder," he said with a meaning look. "I'll see fair play for you."

Auguste Henri, who had continued his draughts intemperately, first turned pale and then blustered and vinously vapoured that he would not go at any man's dictation—he didn't owe any apology to "*ce niais*."

"You've got to go," said Blinders calmly, but with conviction. "You needn't make any apology for insulting him as you did. But you must stand up to the rack, or you can't stay here."

So Blinders quietly led off his man, cursing in French like the rattling of a locomotive. They found Peter Skerrett and Sir Com waiting behind the hill. The latter had his coat off, and was tramping this way and that, like a polar bear in a cage.

"Your name is Pierre Le Valet," said Ambient. "You needn't lie about it. Skewwett, show Blinders the handkerchief. I've been sure for some time you were one of those damn thieves that gouged me in Pawis. Now I know it by your looks and by that name. You've behaved like a blackguard to-day, and I'm going to lick you, if I can, on the spot. You know, Blinders, what the fellow has been doing here—cheating evewybody."

"Take off your coat, Mr. Le Valet," said Blinders, "and thank your stars you've one gentleman to thrash you and another to stand by and see you're not killed."

The detected blackleg made a treacherous rush at Ambient, furious and intending to try some shabby trick of a *savate*, but a solid one, two smote his countenance and floored, or rather, turfed him. As he did not come up to time, Ambient took from Blinders a light Malacca joint and wallopped the skulking wretch until he began to scream for mercy. By this time, the facial one, two had developed into two ugly black eyes. "Hot nubbless" was unpresentable, and Peter and Blinders led him off to a boat and sent him away, swearing vengeance spitefully.

"What can he do, Peter?" asked Blinders.

"Harm, I'm afraid, to someone," replied Peter, thinking how he had come into possession of the handkerchief and doubting much whether he had done right to show it. "What shall we say of his absence—that perfidious Albion and proud Gallia had a contest as to who was victor at Waterloo?"

"What have you done with Monsieur De Châteaunéant?" asked Mrs. Budlong, looking sharply at the two, as they walked back.

"He had a bad head," replied Peter innocently, "and thought he would be better at home. We have charged ourselves with his excuses."

After the banquet, Clara and Diana, with the two other members of their quartette, had retired apart from the crowd. It was almost sunset. They had chosen a vantage point of vision just at the summit of a soft slope, commanding the old fort and the bay. The boats lay picturesquely grouped in front. The wash of waves sent up a pleasant, calming music. They were alone, except when some promenading couple passed at the distance. Paulding was lying half-hid by the short sweet-fern bushes, smoking lazily. Clara was near him. Diana and Dunstan were at a little distance, so that a slight modulation of the voice made conversation joint or separate. Diana had been the gay one thus far; but now the pensiveness of evening seemed to quiet her.

"The sky and water and those mossy rocks remind me of Mr. Kensett's pictures," Clara said. "He seems to have been created to paint Newport delightfully."

"Rather Newport for him to paint," corrected Diana, "as the world was made for man, the immortal. Besides, Mr. Kensett is not narrowed to Newport for his subjects. I notice that so many of you who know him speak of him by his prenom. Only very genial men are so fortunate as to be treated with this familiarity, even by their friends."

"He is indeed genial—one of the men whose personal, apart from his artistic life, is for the sunny happiness of those who know him. Apropos of prenoms, Miss Clara," continued Dunstan, "pray what melodious, terminal syllables belong to your father's initial, W.? G. W.—his G. is George, I know. His W. is what?"

"It is an old family name," replied Clara; "Whitegift. My father is fond of genealogy and traces the name to a relative, a Bishop Whitegift."

"An odd name," said Dunstan. "I seem to have heard it before. Ah, now I recollect having read in some old family manuscript that my ancestor, Miles Standish, had some feud with a Pilgrim of that name."

Clara laughed. "You must talk with Mr. Ira Waddy. He has a legend that the first Waddy, Whitegift by name, was cook of the *Mayflower*, and that there grew a feud between him and Miles Standish. The cook put too little pepper in the hero's porridge. Hence an abiding curse, which Mr. Waddy says depressed his branch of the family until his time. He represents the democratic side of our history. My father rather scoffs at the legend. I must tell him the odd confirmation of it from you. It will shock his aristocratic feelings terribly."

"Bah! for the legend," said Dunstan. "Your ancestors, fair lady, were gods and goddesses of other realms than those dusky and too savoury ones where cooks do reign supreme. But I cannot permit my ancestor's curse to rest longer upon you. In my capacity as his representative, in eldest line, I wave my hand. The curse is revoked, nay, changed to a blessing. The old feud is at an end. It will never be revived between us. We shall never quarrel."

"I hope not," said Clara, and turning away abruptly, she renewed her conversation with Paulding apart.

"You accent the 'we,'" said Diana, "as if you could imagine yourself quarrelling with other women."

"Yes," said he; "why not? But women have always the advantage of us in a quarrel. We can compel a man traitor or wrong-doer to pistol or rifle practice. If he shirks, he becomes a colonist of Coventry. But a woman shelters herself behind her sex and dodges the duello. There ought to be a code of honour for them also."

"There is—in the hearts of the honourable," said she.

"Ah, yes! but who are they? How are we to know them, except by those very tests that we cannot apply until falseness and dishonour on the woman's part will be to us the cause of bitter wrong, such as a man should pay us with his life?"

"So you would challenge the gay deceiver to mortal combat? Weapons, a fan against a pocket-comb, across a skein of sewing-silk. Hail! O Attila! scourge of Flirtationdom! Newport will be depopulated when your plan prevails."

"Depopulated of gay deceivers and their victims. You and I, Miss Clara and Paulding, would be left to weep over the slain and strew their graves with old bouquet leaves. But pity the sorrows of the young heroes, murdered now and unavenged, while their murderesses sing their siren song to annual freshmen."

"But why do your freshmen listen to siren songs?"

"Freshmen love music and are unfamiliar with sirens. And even men no longer so fresh, who have been forced to hear sorrowful songs, may mistake siren song for angel song. Harmony is so rare and so heavenly. We hear it one day, and land. We meet no chilling reception; the siren sings on sweetly. The dewy violet and the thornless rose are still worn and the young heart or the weary heart has but one word more of passion to say. The third and last degree of lovers' lessons waits to be taken, lip to lip. But—*Halte là!* Will you walk out of my parlour?' says the spider to the fly. 'Certainly, fair tarantula, since you insist upon it.' Another freshman is on the threshold, or another not-so-very-fresh may be wooed into the web. Continue, pretty dear, your wanton wiles. Sing away, Siren, seeming angel. We are out. *Adieu!*" and Dunstan, whose cigar was smoked to the thick, drew an immense puff and breathing out a perfect ring, deposited it upon his engagement finger. He held up his hand, while the smoke slowly drifted away in the still, warm air.

Diana laughed. "Very well done, the ring and the description. But the termination was rather too contemptuous for the poetry of the beginning."

"Was it?" said he. "Contempt is not a pleasant feeling. I supposed myself too old to express, if not to have it."

"Did you mean your history," asked Diana, "for the epitaph of a dead love?"

"A dead love? No! Diana, no! It was the *hic jacet* on the cenotaph of a hundred buried flirtations—my own and other men's. Not all of them can chisel the inscription as coolly as I do, nor be as indulgent as I am to the memory of the names inscribed. But love! Love is undying!"

As he said this, they heard a little rustle and a sigh near them. They turned. It was Miss Milly Center. She had heard, perhaps, all the conversation. She rose and seemed about to speak, but her effort ended in something like a sob, and two rather well-made tears started and overran her cheeks.

Just then a cheerful voice came over the hill: "'Oh, Susannah! don't you cry for me——'" and a very shiny glazed hat with a black ribbon, such as is some men's ideal of "the thing" for a head-piece at a water-party, appeared. This hat was on the top of Billy Dulger.

"I was looking for you, Miss Milly," he cried, "and wondering where you had wandered to."

"I'm very glad you have found me," said she. "I don't care to be third in either of these duos."

She had whisked away her tears before she turned to answer Billy Dulger's hail, and now with a smile she took his arm and walked away. But it was not a very happy smile.

Clara and Paulding had not perceived her presence until Dulger appeared; they were too distant to hear the conversation just interrupted, or to observe her confusion.

"Perhaps Miss Center recognised herself in the heroine of your tale," said Diana. "Do you know the hero? It must have happened long ago. I think you have made Mr. Dulger's fortune. He has been a faithful swain, I hear. So you think that, though flirtations may, love cannot die?"

"Diana," he began, and it was the second time he had addressed her thus. He paused; the sun had just set. A flash and burst of white smoke shot from the ramparts of Fort Adams, across the strait. It was the sunset gun. A great, massive, booming crash came over the water, and then, eagerly, tumultuously chasing it, a throng of echoes followed.

"O love, they die in yon rich sky,

They faint on hill or field or river:

Our echoes roll from soul to soul,

And grow forever and forever."

"Diana," continued Dunstan, "let us walk a little."

They went on for a few steps in silence, her arm in his. They had not noticed the direction they took, and these few steps brought them over the crest above the banqueting spot. Several of the party were gathered about Mrs. Wilkes and aiding her in arranging for return.

"Come, Mr. Dunstan," cried Mrs. Wilkes, catching sight of him as he was turning back. "You are just the person I wanted to select Mrs. Wellabout's forks and Mrs. Skibbereen's spoons. No! no! I can't excuse you. Young men must make themselves useful at my picnics. You've had the belle long enough. She must be tired of you by this time. I understand what it means when ladies bring their cavaliers back to the chaperon's neighbourhood."

Dunstan half uttered an ugly Spanish oath. Diana, half-hearing, gave him a reproving look. Belden and another gentleman approached and Dunstan was dragged off to identify spoons and forks. He recognised all his obligations to Mrs. Wilkes, and did his best to help that busy lady through her embarrassments with clumsy servants. He did not even break plates and dishes. Men who have had their California or frontier experience, understand themselves in crockery and cookery. Still, at this moment, he would have preferred not to be so useful.

And now Mrs. Wilkes, like a wise mother of an errant brood, began to sound her homeward notes of recall. The roll of the party began to complete itself. Someone asked, "Where is Diana?" Where, indeed?

"I saw her walking off alone towards the Dumplings some time ago," Gyas Cutus said. "I asked if she wanted a companion and she said no—so I thought I wouldn't go."

"You may go and look for her, Mr. Dunstan," said the chaperon, "as payment for your industry."

Dunstan sprang up and *non scese, no, precipitò* down the hillside. Clara looked anxiously after him. These were the saddening moments of twilight, when sunset glories are gloom and we are not yet quite reconciled to night. Some one of the festal party said that the evening was ominously beautiful—it seemed there could never be another to compare with it. Splendours were exhausted.

The Dumplings stands upon a low, craggy hillock at the water's edge. In front is a bit of precipice; then a scarped slope, covered with débris, such as bricks, stones, broken bottles, sardine boxes, and chicken bones; then rocks again and water. On the landward side the rough hillock is still steep, but overcome by a path circling the crumbling round of the fort. This path is rather up and down, enough so to blow most dowagers and duennas; the ascent has therefore its great uses in the world, and many a tender word has been gasped from panting hearts of those who panted up together, eluding, for precious moments, the stern duenna below.

Dunstan climbed rapidly up. It was but a few steps, yet in the moment all that had ever passed between him and Diana came powerfully back, as all the sounds of a lingering storm are suddenly embodied in one neighbour thunder-clap, and all its playfully terrible lightnings, illuminating scenes far away, concentre in the keen presence and absence of the flash that strikes near by. The evening, whose ominous beauty had impressed him also, was so still that he could hear gushes of gay laughter from the party. He could see nothing of Diana. She must be within the fort. As he stepped along the narrow ledge of the pathway, he checked himself an instant before entering the ruined gateway, and called "Diana!" No answer! Could she have gone elsewhere? He sprang within the inclosure.

Diana was there. She sat leaning against an angle of the crumbling wall. As he entered, she turned towards him a ghastly and agonised face. She did not stir. She was pressing her handkerchief to her arm. He was at her side in an instant.

"Blood! blood again!" he said, with a dreadful shudder. "It shall not part us now—Diana, my love! my love!"

He took her very tenderly in his arms. Blood was flowing freely from a wound in her arm. He tore off his cravat and checked the flow and was binding the place with his handkerchief. The agonised look on her face changed to a smile of gentleness.

"Harry," she said, "this is nothing—a scratch—I fainted and fell. That was the old wound. I am dying with the old wound. Dying to-day, when I was happy again—to-day, when I know you love me still."

"Love you—oh, Diana! I have been waiting through all this long despair for this one moment. I knew the terror must pass away that separated us, and now a new terror comes—the old wound—dying—no! no! Oh, my God!"

He drew back and looked at her. There was no dreary ghastliness in her pallor. He took her in his arms again for one long, lover kiss—one long kiss of life to life and soul to soul. In that kiss all their old hopes were fulfilled; all their old confidence came back again; all doubt and hesitation were gone forever. Fate, that was so cruel to them, forgave them again. The old terror between them had slowly sunk away, like a vanishing, ghostly dream,— vanishing as light of heaven grows strong and clear over the soul. The blood that they knew of on each other's hands was washed and worn away, flowing no longer between, a dark line, narrow but deep as the river of death.

They had riven their last embrace long ago, because a death, bloody and terrible, beheld them with dead, chilling eyes. Even that last embrace, with all its passionate despair, seemed a sacrilege, a repeated parricide. What if the murder was no murder? Then there was the dead. There, studying them with staring eyes, staring beyond them into an eternity of vengeance. Was that a place for love's endearments? For tenderness dear and delicate? No! no! depart! Fly, lover! Seek thy saddest exile! Crush thy dear, dear longings! Forget! ah, yes, forget! That guiltless crime they knew of severed them. Go! Let this impossible love be crushed or forgotten.

Crushed! Forgotten! These despot words are uttered easily; but all the while they know their futileness. Stronger grows mightiness until it has prevailed. And love is the strongest strength. This is the permanent and uncontrollable victor, stronger than death.

But slowly for these lovers the sense of their guiltlessness overcame the awe of crime. Heaven pardons ah! things more guilty far, than their unhappy and bewildered innocence. They saw pardon rising over them, pale but hopeful as the twilight of dawn. And when this pardon overspread their hearts, like the throbbing violet of daybreak, and the pardoned lovers met, how could they know that parting had not done its common work? All common loves are slain by separation. So these two lovers stood apart; each ignorant whether Heaven had been generous to the other of its gift of pardon, and each unwilling, as proud souls may be, to hold the other to old pledges and perhaps detested bonds. Apart, but approaching surely; until the pleasant, meaning playfulness of picnic talk, and the fateful apparition of the flirt, and the chance confession of an old, half-forgotten folly, had revealed to them, clear as their hopes had been, the certainty of their love, unchanged, unchangeable, eternal, infinite.

He had taken Diana in his arms again. Her hurt was surely not grave, a cut upon her arm as she fainted and fell. But again another spasm of paling agony passed over her face.

"The old wound," she said despairingly. "I am fainting again. Take me to Clara."

He lifted her—she, so dying as it seemed—he so strong in his heart's agonies of death.

He did not note it then, but he remembered long afterward, that as he passed from the fort, the moon was rising pale and solemn, through the dull, leaden blush, reflected from sunset upon the misty east.

The gay picnic party had hardly observed Dunstan's brief absence. Clara was watching the fort, and as Dunstan issued with his burden, she ran wildly down the slope. She met them at the foot of the escarpment. Dunstan had found himself staggering at the last few steps and was resting, kneeling by Diana. Clara knelt by his side.

"Dear sister," said Diana, unclosing her eyes, and seeming to revive at her presence. She made a feeble movement with her wounded arm. "It is nothing, dear Clara. But I am suffering from the old pain. Forgive me that I concealed something. I could not tell you all. Now I can, for I have found my old unchanged love. We will rest here a moment. I grow stronger. Perhaps I can walk to the boats. Harry, tell her all our sad story. Dear Clara!"

Dunstan, in a few quick full words, gave Clara the history of their love and their parting. Clara listened, divining much with eager interpretation.

"Dear Diana! Who could have been strong to bear this?" said she. "Why could you not let me comfort you?"

"I thought," said Diana, "that there was to be comfort for me nevermore, until Miss Sullivan was my angel of pardon. Oh, how wise and good she is! My mother—our mother, dear sister."

The unwilling, almost unconscious coldness that had withdrawn Clara from her friend, had utterly passed away. It shamed her now like a crime, that uncontrollable passion had made her an unacknowledged, unperceived rival. But the harm was done, and she must know it bitterly in her heart and endure silently. She kissed Diana tenderly, desolately, and gave her hand to Dunstan. They felt the tenderness: they could not see the desolation.

Paulding, who had been at the boats, bestowing paraphernalia, now appeared, and learning from the party that something was wrong, he came swinging down the slope with giant strides.

"I can walk now," said Diana. "To-day speak to Mr. Paulding and the others only of my fall and the cut; that explains itself. The rest by-and-by," and she smiled hopefully with that beautiful smile, sadder than tears to those who behold it and know the hopelessness of its deceiving consolation.

Paulding came up, followed by Sir Comeguys. Both showed great concern at the accident. Diana thanked them and said that she hoped it was only trifling, though a shock at first. She then walked slowly to the boats, clinging to Dunstan's arm.

Everyone was in such consternation at Diana's accident that she made efforts to recover her usual spirits and partly succeeded. Good Mrs. Wilkes must not be mortified by a calamity at her picnic. All the men who did not venture to be in love with Diana, or who loved elsewhere, liked her, and the ladies were not jealous of so unconscious a belle. She had breadths of sympathy. Miss Milly Center, Queen of the Birthday Festival, came and took Diana's hand softly and was very sorry. And when Diana thanked her gently, poor Milly, on her gay birthday, burst into tears.

In Miss Milly's walk with Mr. Dulger, she had been very exasperating. There was no object she carried that she did not drop, and few that she did not break or tear. Poor Billy was put terribly in fault by her conduct. He could not endure it another day, and when Milly finally crashed her parasol into a bag of silk filled with comminuted whale-bone, and said, "You must have it mended to-morrow before eleven, Mr. Dulger, and bring it to me," he resolved to make the morrow's morn the crisis. It should end for better or for worse, for richer or for poorer, his dumb thraldom. He would kick away the platform and be a dangler no more, even if he broke his neck. Courage, Billy Dulger!

Mr. Belden was especially distressed at the accident. In fact, he seemed, in speaking to Clara, to assume a right to more than friendly sympathy. Clara observed, now for the first time, that singular resemblance between him and Dunstan. She saw why Diana had allowed an intimacy.

Clara, studying Belden's face, quickly and keenly, discovered that the resemblance was not a pleasant one. All her old distrust of him returned.

"Please do not speak of it to-day, Mr. Belden," she thought proper to say to him, "but you will be glad to know that Diana and your friend, Mr. Dunstan, are engaged. It is an old affair revived. It began in Texas a long time ago."

Belden, with his usual self-possession, said what was friendly and commonplace on such occasions. Clara was almost deceived. She could not hear the monosyllable he sent out with a blast, as he turned toward Mrs. De Flournoy.

Admiral Mrs. Wilkes re-embarked her party for the moonlight sail. Except Diana's accident, which that lady made light of to the happy chaperon, everything had gone on and off most prosperously. It was whispered that Titania had accepted Mr. Nicholas Bottom, the millionaire; and poor Cinderella, whom the hostess feared might be neglected, had been walking all day and picking buttercups with Mr. Oberon, the genius.

So with the faint breeze of a silent night of summer, they drifted across the bay, away along the path of moonlight. Song and gay hail and answer passed from boat to boat of the flotilla. Delicious night! Happy world! Fortunate Miss Milly Center, with such a joyous birthday! Kind Mrs. Wilkes! Universal success! Huzza!

At the Millard, Mr. Waddy and Peter Skerrett found Mr. Budlong just arrived. He came up to them with his now anxious manner.

"That beggar of a Frenchman has come home pretty well bunged up," he said. "He has sent word that he wants to see me. I wish you would go, Peter, my boy, and talk to him. I can't guess what it means. If he wants to borrow money, lend him."

Mrs. Budlong came in with Belden. She gave her husband a couple of fingers of welcome. Millard's band was playing and she, with several other untiring females, organised a hop.

Peter Skerrett went off to see De Châteaunéant. It was late when he came down. He found Mr. Waddy waiting on the piazza, his cigar oddly lurid in the mosquitoless moonlight.

"He makes conditions," said Peter, "the infernal shabby wretch! He says if they don't give him Miss Arabella, he'll expose Mrs. Budlong. He pretends to have proofs; and I'm sorry to say that I fear he has them. I could have beaten him to death, the contemptible cuss! if he hadn't been lying there in bed, sick and swelled like a pumpkin. He can't show to-morrow and we shall have all day to work."

"He'll sell out, won't he, Peter?" asked Mr. Waddy. "I haven't contributed to foreign missions yet, and here's an opportunity. We'll try and arrange it to-morrow."

Dunstan called late at Mr. Waddie's. Clara saw him.

"Diana is doing well," she said. "We will have good hope," and in her fair beauty by the moonlight she seemed to him an angel of hope. He could not see her tears as she turned away and fled from him, and from herself, to Diana's bedside.

All night he walked and wandered on the cliffs, watching the light in Diana's window. Sometimes he thought he saw another figure wandering like himself; but always when he approached, he found some uncertain deceptive object, shrub or rock. He was alone in the moonlight, with his memories, his hopes, his despairs. Alone in the wide world with his love. Dying? No! He would not interpret thus the melancholy fall of waves.

Mr. Belden was rather late that night. He had been walking somewhere with Mrs. Budlong—very late somewhere with Mrs. Budlong; he sat in his room reflecting.

"Hell!" said he again. "I've lost the Diana chance, whether she meant to cheat me or not. Well, I'm sure of my bet on the race; and if the worst comes to the worst, I'm glad to know that Betty Bud has some money of her own. I'm sure of her. That job is done."

I am afraid Belden was becoming a very vulgar ruffian. He had very soon, in coarser amours, drowned his first disappointment for the loss of Diana.

CHAPTER XX
CHIN CHIN AND PETER SKERRETT SEIZE THE FORELOCK OF OPPORTUNITY

MR. DULGER arose in the morning dull and early. He stood several hours over the industrious prolétaire who was mending Miss Center's parasol. Meantime Billy smoked weak cigars, pulled at his sporadic moustache, and studied at a formula of words he meant to use, but would forget.

At eleven, he might have been seen walking in Millard's halls, uneasily, with a neat parasol in hand.

At 11.03, Miss Millicent descended Jacob's Ladder equipped for a walk. She was evidently oblivious of her appointment, and taking no notice of poor Dulger at the lower turn of his beat, she turned into the parlour and sat there quite alone, playing with her gloves. Surely she was waiting for someone.

Trepidatingly Dulger approached—— When they returned from their walk, an hour afterward, it was announced, proclaimed, thundered, through Millard's and through Newport, that Miss Center and Mr. Dulger were engaged. Bulletins to that effect were dispatched to postoffices from the Aroostook to the Rio Grande, as members of Congress say. Billy telegraphed to his friend, the bookkeeper, to send a thousand-dollar diamond ring from Tiffany's by express; it came, and glittered on her finger that evening at the hop. Billy's investment for the ring was one-tenth of one per cent. on her million, and, *certes*, was not extravagant. Rich Milly! Poor Milly! Poor Dulger! Rich Dulger! Poor, rich Mr. and Mrs. Dulger!—the man never forgetting his long and sulky apprenticeship—the woman, unapproached any more by exhilarating flirtations, and never forgetting that her yielding was part compunction and part pis-allerage. So ends the Billy-dulgerid.

Dunstan came down to inquire about to-morrow's race. Mr. Waddy begged him not to withdraw, unless Diana's condition should be critical. No one else could ride Pallid. Peter Skerrett, in search of Mr. Waddy, came up and mentioned the new engagement. No one was surprised.

"It was as sure as shooting," said Gyas Cutus. "He treed her. I gaads! I knew she'd have to come down. He's been lamming her with bouquets ever since she came out."

"And now," says Peter, "she has come down in a shower of gold, reversing the fable of *Danae*."

"There's no fable about the million," said Cloanthus. "I wonder if Billy would lend me a V on the strength of it?"

"I think it's a case of *dépit amoureux*," whispered to Dunstan, Peter Skerrett, penetrating sage.

Dunstan said nothing, and presently walked off. This gossip was distressing to him; he could only think of his love regained, his love perhaps dying. He must not see her that day. Absolute repose was necessary.

"The old wound," he thought; "the old wound," and thinking of it, he shuddered again.

Peter Skerrett took Mr. Waddy's arm, and walked him away to a quiet corner.

"That damned scoundrel of a Frenchman wouldn't accept your proposition," he began. "He said it was wealth for him, but the infernal coxcomb also said he wanted to range himself and become a virtuous man, and a happy father of a family. He must have the 'fair Arabella, whom he loved and whom he believed was secluded from him by the decree of a harsh parent'; some such stuff he uttered and then blew a kiss from his bruised, swelled lips. Faugh!"

Mr. Waddy echoed the exclamation; he shared in all Peter's disgust, and all his anxiety.

"It's lucky," continued Peter, "he can't come out to-day. Everyone's inquiring about the row, and Sir Comeguys says he will only keep still until the fellow is out of bed and able to speak for himself."

"Well," said Waddy, as Peter paused again, "what's to be done? Is that all the scoundrel said?"

"Not by a blamed sight; but it's so damned unpleasant I hate to repeat it. After refusing your offer, he repeated his threat of exposing Mrs. B., and he gave me details. He said he wanted to see her, and if he sent a waiter, she would have to come. I knew that would never do, so I bullied him a little and said I would see her myself. By Jove! think what a box I was getting into. Mrs. B. is cool; perhaps I may as well put it, brassy. She was complimentary enough to say that she was surprised a man of my experience should listen to the idle talk of a man bruised and angry; that possibly Arabella (blinking entirely the question, as touching herself—I had stated his threat as delicately as I could) had given him so much encouragement as to persuade him he had rights. Very probably, for she herself had hoped that he and Arabella would make a match, and still hoped it. As to the slanders of that young brute of an Englishman, they were pure jealousy. She was satisfied of De Châteaunéant's position, and thought his abuser a vile coward for profiting by his personal strength to put a rival out of the way. She would talk over the matter with Arabella and see me in an hour."

"Yes?" said Waddy encouragingly, as Peter paused again, choked with rage. He rather wondered at Peter's emotion, for that gentleman usually held himself well in hand—but then this was an extraordinary case.

"Well," continued Peter, "in an hour, I happened to pass through the corridor. Arabella, cried to a perfect jelly, was just opening the door for her mother. How the harridan must have been bullying that poor girl! And yet she was as cool, and smiling, and handsome, as if she was coming out of St. Aspasia's after her Sunday afternoon nap. She said she had found a little proper ladylike hesitation on the part of Miss Arabella; that young ladies did not like this courting by proxy; and that she had no doubt that when De Châteaunéant was able to plead his own cause, that her daughter's long-existing inclination for him would develop immediately into the desirable degree of affection. By Jove! I couldn't help admiring the woman as she stood and told me all this, perfectly self-possessed, though she knew I believed it was every word a lie. Then she said that, as I was quite the confidential friend of the family, she would ask me to go with her to M. De Châteaunéant. And I went! What do you think of that, Waddy?"

"I don't know what to think," answered Ira. "And yet it was probably the best thing to do."

"So I thought," agreed Peter. "She sat down by the beggar's bedside and told him, by Jove! that she thought he needed a little motherly sympathy; that she had always looked with great favour upon his suit for her daughter, and that she hoped and had no doubt the young lady would smile upon him. She could promise it, in fact, after an interview this morning. I tell you, Waddy, she took my breath away. I could have screamed with laughter."

"No doubt," said Mr. Waddy grimly. "How did the farce end?"

"It ended with a few minutes' earnest whispering on the part of the lady. Then she got up triumphantly, and that blackguard turned his ugly swollen face towards me.

"'Monsieur Skarrette,' he said, in his dirty, broken English, 'I veel vate faur ze promesse auf Mees Arabella teele aftare to-morrah. I veel not be anie maur cheete. Ef she do not agree, I sall tale all to Meestare Buddilung.'

"Well," continued Peter, "I was white hot—I don't think I shall be ever quite so angry again—I certainly hope not. I think Mrs. B. saw it and feared some further injury to the Gaul, for she said good-bye hastily and carried me away with her. Out in the hall, she turned to me again, cool as a cucumber.

"'You see he is quite reasonable,' she said, with amazing impudence, 'though naturally rather ardent for his object. We are much obliged to you, Mr. Skerrett.'

"She gave me her hand and the only sign of emotion she showed in the whole interview was to grasp mine like a vice. A few minutes afterward, I saw Belden help her into his buggy and they drove off together. Do you suppose it possible that she meditates some escapade with him? Of course all this couldn't be told to poor old Flirney; he should be saved, if possible. But I could not bear to think of Arabella being the victim of such an infernal plot, without a friend. The matter had gone too far for ceremony, so I went up and knocked at her door. There is so much of that familiarity going on, that I supposed no one would notice it. She opened the door and, when she saw me, burst into tears. I felt so sorry for the poor child that I couldn't help——"

"Oh, you did, did you?" interrupted Ira, seeing a great light.

"Yes, I did; and she shall be Mrs. Peter Skerrett, if her step-mother is a—— She shall, by Jove!"

"Peter, you're the king of trumps!" cried Mr. Waddy, and held out his hand. "And, by curry! you deserve to be congratulated. She's a nice girl."

"She is!" agreed Peter, with conviction. "I've known it a long time. Well, to return, the poor thing was actually bewildered with terror. She said that she liked the fellow well enough at first—you know he has the talents of an adventurer—he flattered her and led her on, always speaking French, until he had got up a great intimacy. Then Mrs. Budlong,—she no longer called her mother,—began to persuade her to accept him, and then to treat the matter as settled; and then to bully her and say that her honour was engaged, and her character would be gone if she did not marry him.

"Imagine the poor girl, so young, and totally uneducated to think for herself, in the grasp of that infernal crocodile! Then her brother, that mean little squirt, Tim, made some heavy gambling debts to the Frenchman, and he told her he thought the marriage was just the thing, and wouldn't listen to a word from her. Mrs. Budlong said that her father had given his full approval to the match. Arabella felt utterly abandoned, and I do believe that horrid hag would have carried her point before this, if Ambient hadn't stepped in with his timely licking. At the picnic the Frenchman was continuing to treat her with tyrannical familiarity. She hated him so much that she longed to go to Diana and Clara for protection, but she feared they would think her a silly little snob and send her to her mother. Mother!" repeated Peter with emotion, and swallowed hard.

Mr. Waddy also felt an unaccustomed lump in his gullet.

"Peter," said he, a little huskily, "I'm proud of you. By Jove! I'm proud to know you. You're the best man in the lot. The rest of us would have stood around and seen that girl sent to the devil and never have lifted a finger to prevent it."

"Oh, come," protested Peter, "I know better than that. And then, besides, you see, you—you didn't have my incentive. She needed someone, Waddy; she said she'd always thought me one of her best friends—but she couldn't speak to any gentleman about her troubles, much less me. And then she began to cry again and I had to kiss her again like a brother and tell her that I was her best friend and would save her. Luckily, no one happened to pass; so I let her sob herself quiet in my arms and told her to have courage and not to speak to anyone on this subject. What a damnable infamy it is! I don't care for Mrs. Budlong, and would let her be exposed and go to the devil, but it will kill the old gentleman. He's a good old boy, and actually loves that woman. We must save him if we can. Here is old Mellasys, Saccharissa's father; couldn't we get him to kidnap the Frenchman for a fugitive slave?"

"Peter," said Waddy, "we may get the Frenchman off, but there is left behind a man much more dangerous than any Frenchman—Belden!"

About eight o'clock that evening, Mr. Waddy sent Chin Chin to inquire of Diana's health. On his return, Chin Chin made a circuit to a shop he knew of. His object was lager beer, a washy beverage, favoured by Chinamen, Germans, and such like plebeian and uncouth populaces. Feeling sleepy after his draught, he gradually subsided into a ball and sank under the table. Except, perhaps, Box Brown and Samuel Adams, packed some years ago by John C. Colt, corner Broadway and Chambers Street, no being is known, bigger than an armadillo or a hedgehog, capable of such compact storage as a slumbering Chinaman.

Chin Chin under the table was therefore not perceived by two men who came in to get beer and mutter confidences over it. He, however, waking and craftily not stirring until he could do so without disturbing legs endowed with capacity to kick, heard this secret parley. He could not recognise the legs, but could the voices.

As soon as he was released, he ran to the Millard, and gave his message to Mr. Waddy; then, in consequence of the beer-shop discoveries, he crept along like a quick snake to his master's hired stable. The night was very dark, the clouds obstructing the moon. Chin Chin's mission and his plan were perfectly suited to his crafty Malayan nature. He knew the stable intimately. He had often found it a handy place to snooze away the effects of beer or gluttony—larger and more airy than his usual habitation, and much less liable to rude invasion. He had prepared a secret means of ingress and egress; now, after a quick glance around, he glided along to one corner, moved a board slightly and crept inside through the crevice thus revealed.

In the stable were Mr. Waddy's three horses. Pallid stood next to a vacant stall. A roughly contrived manger, with no division, passed through all the stalls. The back door of the stable opened upon a yard, separated by a low fence from a dark lane. There was a locked door through this fence; both the stable doors were also locked.

Pallid recognised the Chinaman and whinnied a welcome nearly as articulate as the other's reply. Chin Chin's plan was already laid. He did not seem to need light to execute it. He groped about for a billet of wood in a spot he knew of, and drawing a fine fishing line from his pocket, made it fast to the billet, which he then threw over a beam running the length of the stable. He drew the billet up to the beam by his line, and holding the end, wormed himself in under a heap of hay that filled the stall next to Pallid's. He found that, without changing his position, he could pass his hand into the adjoining manger. It seemed he had a fancy of possible danger, for he took from his breast pocket a perilous piratical knife and laid it in the manger at his side.

"Pigeon—all same—Hi yah!" said he, with gleaming teeth and a grin.

Chin Chin waited, probably dreaming of the Central Flowery Land and fancying himself under the shade of his native tea plant, offering a tidbit of rat pie to the fair Pettitoes in sabots, skewered hair, talon finger-nails, and brocaded raiment.

His tender, nostalgic reverie was disturbed by the cautious turning of a key. The door opened and two men armed with a slide lantern entered. They drew up the slide and stood revealed, a precious pair, Belden and Figgins, come to superintend the training of Pallid for to-morrow's race.

They peered cautiously round the stable—nothing but horses and hay. They could not see that snake-in-the-grass watching them with glittering eye and keen delight.

"We must do it quick, Figgy," said Belden; "give me the ball. You hold the light. Whoa, Pallid!"

He stepped to the stall, and patting Pallid on the neck, placed a very suspicious-looking horse-ball in the manger. Pallid was beginning to turn it over and sniff at it, when—slam, bang!—Chin Chin let go the billet. It crashed to the floor, knocking down sundry objects with a terrible clatter.

The conspirators started, looked at each other fearfully, and sprang back as if to escape. The noise ceasing, they looked about with anxiety. Belden caught sight of the billet and its effects.

"Bah!" said he. "Nothing but a stick of wood fallen down——" and turned back to the horse.

Meantime, under cover of the noise and panic, Chin Chin had snatched away the dosed sausage from Pallid's manger, and thrown in a handful of oats. The horse champed them.

"The greedy brute has swallowed his pill and is licking his damned chops," Belden announced. "Well, you black devil, so much for you for throwing me, and so much for your master. You won't win any race to-morrow nor this year."

Again examining suspiciously everywhere, they went out as cautiously as they had entered.

Chin Chin chuckled. He was fond of Pallid and fond of the turf, a novel fancy for a Chinaman. He knew if he revealed this adventure to Mr. Waddy, that the race would come to an end, so far as that gentleman was concerned, at least. Chin Chin wanted to see the fun. Unluckily for Figgins, he had bets with him. Chin Chin determined to consider himself the executive of retribution and keep his own counsel till after the race. He looked at the ball; he smelt it.

"Pose good for Chinaman," he said, "ebryting all same pigeon eat em rat; eat em puppy; pose eat em sossidge. Hi yah! first chop good, all same."

He nibbled a little bit, ate a little bit, and then looking out and finding the coast clear, cautiously crept homeward in the shadow. As he ate, he seemed at first very well satisfied, then less satisfied, and finally not at all satisfied, and throwing away the remnants of the ball, he made for the Millard, pressing both his hands on that part of his person which seemed the centre of dissatisfaction.

CHAPTER XXI
THE STORY OF DIANA AND ENDYMION

DIANA was still very ill. They found it necessary to keep her perfectly quiet. The old wound, never fully healed, had given her much pain of late. Mental excitement at the picnic and her fall had produced feverish symptoms. Her physician had fears which he hardly ventured to express; which he hardly dared formulate, even to himself. She had aroused herself enough during the day to send a kind message by Clara to Dunstan, and to ask that they would write to Miss Sullivan to come on. A letter to that lady would go by the morning mail to Boston.

Dunstan was in an agony of suspense. During the day, he tried to distract his fixed madness of thought by training Pallid over the beach. The other men were also out on the beach or the road. Bets were nearly even on Pallid, Knockknees, and Nosegay. Toward evening, Dunstan mounted his own horse and galloped off up the island. The wild sunset and windy drift of torn, black clouds was such a mood of nature as suited the terror at his heart. It was a night like this when, in Texas, he had started from San Antonio to ride sixty miles across the country and catch his train. There were such stormy masses of weird clouds, so flashed through by an August moon, so floating at midnight, when, as he dashed along the trail, shouting in savage exhilaration, all the wildness of his nature bursting forth in mad songs and chants of Indian war, suddenly his trusty horse, who had borne him thousands of miles in safety by night and day, over deserts of dust and wastes of snow, fell with him, on him, crushing him terribly. And then, by just such fitful gleams of moonlight, he had dragged himself desolately along, with unbroken limbs, but mangled and bleeding—dragged himself whither he saw a midnight lamp, as of one who watched the sick or the dead. And near the spot whence the light came, he had sunk voiceless, fainting, dying, until he was awakened by a tender touch upon his brow, and saw bending over him, in the clear quiet of midnight, Diana, who had found at last and was to save her Endymion: Diana, from that moment to become the passion of his every instinct, the love of every thought.

But now, now it was she who was the wounded, the fainted, the dying. O God! he could not think of this despair, and he cried aloud and galloped on furiously. The drift of wild black clouds followed him as he rode and met him more gloomily as he returned.

He could not rest, and soon resumed his sentinel tramp along the shore. There for hours he walked, the breakers counting his moments drearily. The horizon all to seaward was a black line, and over it the sky was lurid blankness; it did not tempt the voyaging hope to circle ocean, chasing distant dawn. He could not seek a refuge for his miserable hopelessness in that reasoning with the infinite called prayer. Was it to make him happy or content that men, questioning the infinite and receiving for all answer, "Mystery!" had essayed for themselves to interpret this dim oracle and had feigned to find that sorrows and agonies are strengthening blessings? So the happy and the placid say: so say not the lonely and bereaved. Pain is an accursed wrong, for all our self-beguiling and self-flattery in its lulls.

This was a man of thorough, tested manhood. There was no experience that educates the body and the mind which he had not proved. All this preparation was done; he was facing the duties of his full manhood. And now that was to happen, that sorrow he knew must come, which would make every effort joyless, every achievement a vanity, every belief a doubt, every day sick for its coming night of darkness, and every morn sad for its uninvited dawning and eager for speedy night.

As he moved along the shore, he was aware again, as on the previous night, of a shadow lurking in the dimness.

"Possibly a mischief-maker," he thought, and half-concealing himself, he waited to watch. The figure approached—a man. He stepped forward to meet him in the moonlight.

"Paulding!"

"Dunstan!"

The two friends had not met since the picnic. Paulding knew, only as everyone now knew, that his friend and Diana were engaged. He therefore could conceive why there was one night wanderer by the shore. In a few passionate words, he told Dunstan his own secret—the secret of his sorrowful unrest. He, too, loved Diana.

"My dear friend," said Dunstan tenderly, as the other sobbed and was silent, "I have seemed almost a traitor to you and if I could have dreamed of this, I would have even violated my pledge to tell you before what I now can tell permittedly. I was too busy with my own happiness in recovering Diana to think of any other man or woman."

"Recovering her?" repeated Paulding. "Then you had already met——"

"Yes," said Dunstan, and recounted the incident of his night ride from San Antonio and his fall. "Diana went out upon the lawn," he continued, "to study the moon, her emblem. She heard my moans. The noble woman was living there alone with her mother, once ruined and mad, and now dying. Her whole household consisted of a few negroes and two or three Mexican servants. When I awoke from my fainting fit and found her stooping over me, I knew in that moment that she was to be the goddess of my life. Love came upon me like a revelation. She had me taken to her house, and herself dressed my wounds and cared for me. You know her dignity and judgment as a woman of society, but you may hardly imagine the energy and skill and contrivance and fearless delicacy she showed in her treatment of me, as I lay there a perfectly helpless invalid. I convalesced slowly. We found that our worlds of society and thought and aspiration were the same. The circumstances were what are called romantic. I need not give you the history of my growing love. You know the woman. You know the man. It was fate. Anywhere it must have been the same; there, how doubly certain. I have never known any being like Diana; fresh and free and fearless as a savage, and yet the heir of the beautiful refinements of all chivalric ages. Oh, Paulding—when I think of her, as I knew her then, with a mind and character of an empress, and her dear tenderness of heart, as I knew her and loved her then, and shall forever, I cannot let her die!"

He groaned and was silent for a while. The melancholy crash of breakers undertoned his story, and now, as he paused, it filled the interval like the unpeaceful symphony of some great genius, wasting itself in doleful music.

"Diana had collected in that distant seclusion," he went on, "all the beautiful necessities of elegant life. We had books and music. Our acquaintance, friendship, love marched strong and fast. It grew with my convalescence. It was now admitted love. She had told me the whole of her mother's sad story. Her mother was dying; in days, weeks, or months it would be all over. She besought me to remain and not leave her alone with death. I had never seen her mother, who was confined entirely to her bed.

"You remember that beautiful bowie knife you gave me in California. One day I was sitting on the piazza cleaning that and my six-shooter, for the first time since my fall. I had given the knife an edge keen as a gleam and was trying it on a chip. Suddenly Diana ran out to me. Her mother was wild, she said, almost in convulsions. The old nurse was terrified to death; would I come quick and aid them? She was still speaking, when a mad, ghastly figure, in white, sprang forward and seized her.

"'Devil!' screamed this maniac, 'you shall not ruin my child, as you have ruined me,' and she stabbed Diana furiously in the side with a knife. Then she leaped upon me. I had the bowie in my hand. There was an instant's struggle. I felt her cutting at my neck. I was not aware of using my weapon, but she stiffened in my arms and sank away, bloody and wounded. She died there in a moment, horribly—she, Diana's mother!

"Diana had fallen fainting, but not unconscious—she had seen the whole. I sprang to her. She repelled me with a look of horror. I was covered with blood, my own, her mother's, hers. I screamed for help. The old nurse came out, crouching with terror. Diana dragged herself away, turning back to give me a glance of utter agony.

"I was left alone with the corpse; I washed my own wounds; they were but trifling. I longed for death. I seemed to myself an assassin. I set myself to remove the traces of the struggle. The old nurse came out and aided me, cowering and shrinking away as I touched her. We carried the poor, lifeless body in—Diana's mother, feebly like her daughter. Diana joined us, pale to death. She gave me her hand solemnly.

"'Go,' she said, 'this is between us forever—between me and my undying love. I am better. Do not fear for me. Go. God save and pardon us. Let this be a secret between us and Him.'

"I crept away like a guilty man. My horse had recovered from his sprain; I rode off and left him with the nearest settler, five miles from her house. I returned and lurked like a wild beast in the woods. I saw the funeral. No one was present but her own people. She was pale, but calm and strong. I must fly despairfully, and on my hands the stain of her mother's blood.

"My friend, the settler, told me as a piece of general indifferent news that the madwoman up at the big house had killed herself in a fit. That was the accepted story and went uncontradicted. Soon after, I joined you in New York.

"That is my story. You can imagine the gradual calming of our minds, as we recognised our real guiltlessness. You can understand why, to escape questions, we seemed not to know each other. We learnt in our daily meetings here that we need not shrink from a new friendship, and then, by a chance confidence at the picnic, that our love was unchanged.

"And now, Paulding, forgive this unwilling reticence of mine. You know what was this old wound. I fear the worst. But that we will not speak of."

"It is a wide world, Harry," said Paulding. "There is room in it for many exiles. I shall find my home for wandering—somewhere—anywhere."

The moon sank away drearily, leaving a ghastly paleness in the west. And the melancholy breakers, in darkness now, went on falling, hesitating, lifting, falling on the black rocks, counting the measures of a desolate eternity.

CHAPTER XXII
IN WHICH MR. BELDEN REACHES THE END
OF HIS ROPE

WHEN Mr. Waddy rang his bell in the morning after the stable scene, no Chin Chin appeared, and inquiry developed the fact that Chin Chin was sick. Ira's toilet may, therefore, not have been quite so accurate as usual, and the polish on his neat calfskins not so mirrorlike. In fact, he had too many anxieties crowding around, to concern himself much with cravat ties and the gleaming boot. He sent his groom, a Bowery boy, *pur sang*, to care for Chin Chin.

"He ain't dangerous, sir," that worthy returned to report, "but he's been a-gulpin' down suthin' as has kicked up a bobbery in his innards."

"Very well," said Mr. Waddy; "have Pallid ready for eleven o'clock. How does he look this morning?"

"He's as gay, sir, as a house afire," Bowery assured him. "Yer kin bet yer life on it, he'll rake 'em down!" and Bowery departed, humming cheerfully to himself, confident of being richer ere the day was over.

Major Granby dropped in upon his friend a moment later.

"I'm losing my interest in this race," said Waddy, "since Dunstan's unwillingness to ride has become so evident. Poor fellow! I'm afraid there's very little hope for Diana."

"Don't say so," protested Granby; "the world cannot spare that noble girl. I was just speaking with Skerrett of her. He says she is the only woman he ever knew who is afraid of neither fresh air nor sunshine. And Clara—how can that beautiful friendship be severed? You can hardly imagine how those sisters have quartered themselves in my rusty old heart. Did you ever hear them speak of Miss Sullivan, their governess? She must be a remarkable person."

"Sullivan? No," said Waddy, connecting the name at once with his preserver at The Island. "A lady of that name did me a service once. I must ask them about her."

"Dunstan will ride without fail, I suppose?" asked Granby. "We must beat that fellow Belden."

"Dunstan will hold to his word; if it were to drive the chariot of Tullia," answered Ira, who had read his friend's character aright.

Mrs. Budlong had an interview with Arabella early that morning. Arabella looked very tearful, but there was also a new expression in her face, thanks to Peter Skerrett—one might almost call it determination.

"Well, my dear," said the step-mother, "what shall I say to the lover? He is eager for the kind word of encouragement," and Mrs. De Flournoy played affectionately with the young lady's curls.

"Tell him I hate him!" cried the poor penitent, bursting into tears again. "I hope, madam, you will never mention his name to me—no, not once more! Oh! oh! you hurt me."

The affectionate mamma had given the curls a little tug.

"You silly fool!" said she, "don't you know he can ruin your prospects? You'll offend your father so that he'll discard you, and then what will you do? If you are so dishonourable and disobedient, when we are striving for your good, we shall let you go to the destruction you choose."

"I hope I shall find some friends who will not think me dishonourable," sobbed poor Arabella, thinking with rueful gratitude and confidence of honest Peter and his fraternal feelings. "I'm not dishonourable. I'm trying to do right. I may have been foolish, but that—man—he can't be a gentleman, or he would not persecute me so. I don't know what reason you can have for wanting to make me miserable."

"My reasons are of course wise and judicious," retorted Mrs. B. "I will see you once more, and then, if you do not choose to yield, you will be the cause of the *éclatant* scandal of the season. You won't think of going to the race with those red eyes. I wouldn't take you if you did."

Poor Arabella was the only one who did not go; everybody went; all that we have encountered in this history and platoons of others.

The first beach at Newport is straightish, and a mile or so in length,—a very long "or so," when you are dragged over it in the unwilling family coach, by stagnant steeds—a very short mile when the beautiful comrade whose presence is a consecration and a poet's dream, says "Shall we gallop?" and cheats with fleeting transport, as she passes, the winds from summer seas, that sigh to stay and dally with her curls.

Between beach number one and beach number two is an interregnum of up and down, a regency of dust. Then comes the glorious second beach. You will hardly see anything more beautiful than this long, graceful sweep, silvery grey in the sunshine, with a keener silver dashed along its edge by curving wave that follows curving wave. You will hardly see any place gayer than this same wide path beside the exhilarating dash of the Atlantic, on a gay afternoon of August—hundreds of carriages, more or less well-appointed; scores of riders, more or less well-mounted or -seated.

Thus, then, to the second beach between grey rocks, grey sand slopes, and grey meadows beyond, and on the other hand the gleaming glory of the sea, came at eleven that morning, to see the race, all the snobs and all the nobs. Peter Skerrett and his aides marshalled them. Mrs. Budlong, alone in her carriage, bowed and smiled very pleasantly to Peter. However critical that person may have felt her position, and whatever desperate resolve she might entertain for escape, through whatever postern, from the infamy of public dismissal, she was quite as usual. No; she was even handsomer than usual, more quietly splendid in attire, and reclining with calmer luxuriousness of demeanour on her cushions of satin.

Among the many traps, drags, and go-carts, of various degrees of knowingness, Mr. Waddy's was conspicuous. Major Granby, old Budlong, and Paulding accompanied him. Old Bud said it made him quite young again to see the boys out.

"But, sir," he added, "why do they bump on the outside of a horse, when they might sit and grow fat in a buggy? There's Tim, sir, my boy Tim, is growing quite thin and haggard; he says riding don't agree with him. I'm afraid he won't do much with Drummer to-day."

A straight race, on a dead level, lacks features of varied brilliancy. Peter Skerrett had arranged that the field should start alternately from either end, that all might see alphas and omegas. Thus the proud and numerous start and the disarrayed and disappointed finishes might be viewed by all spectators. All might share the breathless sympathies of doubts and enthusiasms for the winner.

Peter Skerrett, too busy to think of poor Arabella, who, in her bower, was thinking much of him and sighing as she thought how unworthy she had been in her long education of vanities and follies; Peter now brought forward his rank of equestrians. The sea was still, and hardly rustled as it crept along the sands, unterrifying to horse or man; yet the air was cool and the sun not too ardent to be repelled by a parasol.

As the line formed, the ladies chose their champion men and bet gloves recklessly on them; the gentlemen chose champion horses, with a view also to riders, and bet reckfully.

It appeared that Tim Budlong was—bluntly—drunk, and Drummer lost his backers. There was a murmur of sympathy as Dunstan rode up on Pallid; sympathy admiring for this pair, a best of the animal and a best of the man, and sympathy pitiful for the man of a soul that must bear the anxiety and perhaps the sorrow that all knew of. A noble fellow and a generous the common suffrage made him, already distinguished for bold ability and frank disdain of cowardice and paltering. When experience had made him a little more indulgent to the limping progress and feeble vision and awkward drill of mankind, rank and file, he would be a great popular leader. So thought the Nestors, feeling themselves fired by the fervours of this young Achilles.

Belden had overdone his costume, as such men often do. It was urgent with him to look young; he achieved only a gaudy autumnal bloom. Knockknees, *malgré* that ungainly quality of his legs, was an imposing, masculine style of horse. As he passed, stopping to speak intimately to Mrs. De Flournoy, several of the intuitionless women envied that person and several men called him "lucky dog."

Blinders was not a lady's man. His horse was, however, one of the favourites. Very few men but Blinders would have ventured to mount, or even approach, such a rascal brute. Nosegay knew that his master was invincible, but he wished to inform him that they were a pair of invincibles; accordingly, despising the two snaffles, the one in hand, the other around the rider's waist for steady drag, Nosegay would fling his head about and then move on without reference to requests that he tarry or stand at ease.

"That there 'oss'll overrun 'isself," said Figgins to Mr. Waddy's Bowery Boy, with whom he had bets on Pallid, money up. "'E'll make a four-mile 'eat hout of hevery mile 'eat."

"Gaaz, Johnny Bull!" returned the Bowery. "Thar ain't no hoss in a hide as kin git away from Mr. Blinders. It caan't be did. He's one er the bohoys, he is."

Bob O'Link's horse was a mare. The sentimental fellow had named her Lalla Rookh. She was a delicate beauty, but it was quite evident that her master would not give himself the trouble to win.

Scalper was so busy caricaturing Billy Dulger that he was near forgetting to present himself with Gossoon. Little Skibbereen recalled him to his duty. Skibby wanted to see his horse go, and could hardly forgive his mamma for keeping him at her side.

"Why shouldn't I break my neck, ma, if I like?" he protested. "I'll go and break it the day I'm twenty-one and leave my property to the Tract Society."

Sir Com Ambient said good-naturedly that he merely started to make one more in the field. This was clear to the observing eye.

Billy Dulger, having achieved his heart's desire, rode up very unwillingly. The bookkeeper had sent him on garments much too refulgent for this, or any occasion. He was rather conspicuous *per se* as the Great Accepted of Miss Center. The Billy-dulgerid epic, having already been brought to its finale, nothing more need be said of its hero's performances in the race, except that his horse did not disappoint the stableman, his owner; did not win a heat; did not start a second time; and that Billy's hair was full of sand for several days after this eventful one.

Preparations are of years, acts of moments. To run a mile takes a minute and so many seconds, disappointingly brief. Poor, dissolute Tim Budlong, over-fortified by drink, struck Drummer viciously at starting. Drummer shied toward the water and Tim went over his head. Sobered by the plunge, Timothy mounted the horse, which someone caught, and disappeared homeward, fully ashamed of himself.

In a minute and so many seconds, a hurrah came down the wind. Blinders had won; Pallid second; Knockknees third.

"All right next time," telegraphed Figgins to his master.

Sir Comeguys had saved his distance handsomely and now withdrew.

Time was about to be called again. Where was Blinders? At last he reappeared. Nosegay had gone on indefinitely and was at last, with difficulty, persuaded to return.

Off they all go once more. The ladies at the upper end are almost terrified at this assault of cavalry. So even seems the front of charge that all are deemed winners; but the judges announce Pallid first; Knockknees second; Nosegay third—all very close running.

Belden began to be anxious. Instead of drooping, Pallid was improving. Had the poison failed? He superintended the care of his horse most sedulously. Each of the gentlemen had a groom at either end of the course. Dunstan grew excited with success. The match was a very even one. Good riding would determine it. Bob O'Link strolled up to Miss Anthrope's carriage.

"I think I'll win the next heat, if you wish it," said he languidly.

Everyone was astonished at the next announcement of victory. Lalla Rookh first; Knockknees second; Pallid and Nosegay third. Blinders kept Nosegay up, but he was showing the effects of his stubborn struggles. Belden called Figgins.

"By God!" said he, "you've cheated me; the horse goes better every time. I only got ahead this time by Link's riding in."

"Hi dunno what hit means," protested his accomplice. "Hif I've cheated you, Hi've cheated myself. Hevery penny of mine's hon it. I 'ope 'e'll drop next time."

But he did not drop. There was only half a head between him and Nosegay, but Pallid won the race and immense applause. He was victor in the first regular race ever run on the beach of Newport. Everyone felt that the occasion was important.

For a moment Belden sat his horse like a man dazed. He had been falling a long time—at last he had come to the ground. He had backed Knockknees heavily, besides his bet with Granby. He could not pay. He knew that his Boston creditors would be down to attach his horses for Boston debts; Millard's bill of three figures was lying on his table unpaid.

"That damned Figgins will blow me," he thought. He cursed Dunstan, winner of the race, winner of Diana. "She would have made me a better man," thought he, with a groan of despair. "I shall have to retire for a while. Luckily, I've got hold of someone that I can invite, rather positively, to go along and pay expenses."

The thought nerved him, and he pulled himself together. He dismounted, gave his horse to his supplemental groom, and looking with a pleasant scowl around, walked up to Mrs. Budlong's carriage.

"I find it rather warm, now that the race is over," said that person. "Will you get in and drive home with me?"

So they drove off in very handsome style, admired by the admiring, envied by the envious. Mrs. Budlong complained of a headache, and kept her room the rest of the day.

Wellabout drove Dunstan away. They stopped at Mr. Waddie's. Diana would see her betrothed to-day. His heart sank at the announcement. There was, indeed, no hope; she must die; slowly, sadly, after many days of lingering adieux, and all that divine beauty be no more seen and felt to inspire and to consecrate her neighbour world.

Mr. Waddy, Major Granby, and Peter Skerrett returned at ten that evening from dining at the Skibbereens'. Old Budlong met them in the hall, and they all went up to Mr. Waddy's parlour for a cigar.

Chin Chin had reappeared, looking as unwholesome as a cold buckwheat cake. Retribution for his reticence had overtaken him. He began to tell Ira his story of the stable scene in his odd, broken English. While he was so doing, there was a knock at the door. A woman, Miss Arabella's maid, to see Mr. Skerrett, and the Bowery Boy for Mr. Waddy.

Ira interpreted Chin Chin's tale to the other gentlemen.

"Well," said the Bowery Boy, who had waited with the imperturbableness of his class, "if somebody tried t' pizen the hoss afore, it must be the same chap as has did it now. I found this piece of a ball in the manger, and Pallid's down on his side as dead as Billy Kirby."

At this moment Peter Skerrett returned.

"Send your people away, Waddy," said he. "Mr. Budlong, these gentlemen are friends. We shall need their advice. Your wife and Mr. Belden are missing. They probably went in the Providence boat two hours ago."

For a moment no one spoke. Poor Bud sat staring, his face purple, unable for a breath to comprehend. Then his colour faded, his face fell suddenly into folds and wrinkles. He put down his head and groaned.

Before anyone could find words of consolation, or realise how powerless to console any words must be, there came another knock at the door. It was Figgins, looking more like a ticket-of-leave man than ever. The bow in his legs seemed to have increased.

"My master 'as ran hoff without payin' me hanythink," said he, cringing to Mr. Waddy. "Hi found them papers hamong 'is traps," he continued, laying a packet on the table, "hand seein' as they was marked with yer honour's name, Hi thought yer honour mout give me five dollars fer a savink of 'em."

"So you've been thieving as well as trying to poison," said Ira, as he opened the door. "Here, boys," he called to Chin Chin and Bowery, in the adjoining room. "Lug this beggar off. We'll have him attended to to-morrow."

"Hi yi! All same!" shouted Chin Chin, pouncing upon Figgins, and that worthy was dragged off with a Chinaman at his hair and the Bowery Boy playfully tapping him on the nob.

Mr. Waddy picked up the packet of papers, to toss it after Figgins, but held his hand, with a sudden start of astonishment as his eye caught the indorsement. He stared at it a moment, scarce believing that he saw aright; a swift presentiment shook him, turned him hot, cold——

"Gentlemen," said he, a little hoarsely, "I do not desire to pry into Mr. Belden's private papers, but this parcel is indorsed in my own hand, or a hand that seems my own, as relating to me. I shall take the liberty, in your presence, of ascertaining the contents."

He opened them with trembling fingers: the whole plot burst upon him, foul, damnable, unspeakably vile.

"My God!" thought he. "They showed her these—she could not doubt my own hand. And I have wronged her all these fifteen years! Oh, how I pardon her!"

His hands were trembling still; his eyes were hot with tears—tears of joy, tears of thankfulness——

Old Budlong looked up, with a sudden jerk of the head. His eyes, too, were wet and his hands tremulous.

"Gentlemen," said he, steadying his voice, which would have broken, "I'm an old man, but I've been a kind husband, and as devoted to my wife as I knew how. I sometimes thought she was a little gay and it made me unhappy—but I was old and she was young, and I never thwarted her. She has had everything she wished, and, gentlemen, I loved her like a wife and a daughter. She was a beautiful woman, you know, and I found her very poor, the daughter of one of my old cronies, and I put her where she belonged, among splendid things. I have never seen anything handsomer than she was, gentlemen, and I was proud of her."

He spoke of her as if she were dead, and other lips were quivering, in sympathy with his.

"Perhaps you have thought," he went on, after a moment, with a quiet dignity that was new to him and very touching, "that I was too much away this summer; but when we came back from Europe, she asked me to take a few thousands she had inherited from her uncle and operate with them. So I've been at work for her all summer in that hot town. I paid her over the profits last time I was down, in shares of the Manhattan Bank, a good old stock, twenty-three thousand dollars. I thought perhaps she'd like to feel more independent of the old man. I felt a little vain of the operation, gentlemen, and I said to her, 'You see, Betty dear, your old boy does understand one thing, and that is how to make money for you.' She actually cried at that, she did, gentlemen, and said she was very sorry I'd been away so much, working so hard, and she wished she was good enough for me. That doesn't look like a bad woman," he continued, wiping his eyes. "I can't believe she's bad,—not at heart, my friends,—but you know I'm an old man and a little rough, perhaps, and she didn't like my being proud that I'd come up from a deck-hand on a North River barge. It was to please her that I stopped writing my name Flirney and bought my new house and tried to study French and went to Europe. But it was too late—I was too old—I couldn't change—though God knows I tried!

"I'm sorry on Arabella's account," he added, more calmly. "She's an honest girl, and a pretty girl, and a good girl, too, though I say it, and like her own mother, when we lived down in Pearl Street long ago. Now, nobody will speak to the daughter of an old man whose wife has——" And the broken-hearted old gentleman stopped and wiped his eyes again.

"No! no! Peter Skerrett, lad," he continued, "I know what you mean to say. I love you like a son; but it's no use. My name shall never bring its disgrace upon anyone else.

"And now," he added, rising, "I thank you, gentlemen, for your kind feeling and listening to my childish talk. I'm an old man, you see; but there's some of the old stuff left in me still. I start to-morrow morning and I'll trail him— I'll trail him like an Injun. I've lived mostly in the city since I was a boy, but I used to be pretty good with the old King's arm and I guess he'll find I can hit the size of a man yet. Good-night, gentlemen. Good-night, Peter, my boy."

"Mr. Budlong," said Ira, seizing the old man's hand, "I will go with you. My revenge is older than yours."

Well out of Vanity Fair, Mr. Ira Waddy!

CHAPTER XXIII
A VOYAGE OF UNKNOWN LENGTH

THERE will always be a certain number of respectable, but inexperienced and unattractive men whose wives will prefer others more attractive than their husbands, even to the point of infidelity. The wronged husband, who is often not destitute of embryonic manliness, inquires what he is to do, when he is true and his wife is false?

"Look you, stranger! There is only one thing to do. You must shoot!"

Mr. Budlong did not seem any more like a withered De Flournoy in the pursuit of the fugitives. He was strangely alert, keen, skilful in seizing every clew, but totally indifferent to all other interests. In their long and dismal journeys by day and night, he and Ira Waddy sat side by side; stern, self-possessed, silent save on one single topic, and on that speaking only rarely and of necessity. Travellers for autumn pleasure, travellers returning gaily from gay summerings, saw these two grave, iron men, and were awed by their look of inflexible, deadly purpose. There was a watchful meaning in all their actions. Their monosyllables with each other struck like thrusts of a dagger.

At Providence, the fugitives had disappeared. There are many honest couples journeying at that season, and it was impossible to distinguish the dishonest one. Then, too, Belden's dangerous facility of handwriting made the various names they assumed unrecognisable. He took this precaution before he was aware of pursuit. He became aware of it only by a chance. It was at one of the great railroad centres, where lines of rail interlace each other like a network of nerves. The train with Belden and his companion was just quickening on to speed when a coming train rumbled slowly into the station. Belden was looking from a window and divined why these stern men were leashed together. He saw them and they him: it was a view of a moment and roused them afresh to retrace their steps in unflagging pursuit.

Belden grew very shaky after this. Fear is a terribly wearing thing. With prostration of his morale, physical feebleness began also to come. He felt the consequences of his exhausting life. His hand trembled. You would not have bet upon his snuffing a candle with the pistol he carried. In fact, you would have thought it quite unsafe that he should have a pistol. He might shoot a bystander or himself, as well as an assailant. He played too much with that weapon with his nervous, trembling fingers.

It was very soon discovered between him and his partner that their flight was not a necessity of passion. Each had made a convenience of the other, and it was not long before they knew it with mutual disgust. The *intriguante*, to give her the benefit of all euphemism, found out what a ruined villain she had hired for an escort: and she, in revenge, made him understand her own good reasons for absence before exposure. No very pleasant feeling, then, between this pair—certainly not love—passion exhausted—contempt, disgust, hatred growing—only between them the cohesion of guilt, and now of common terror. Chasing him was the punishment of his last and of his first villainy and most he dreaded the older vengeance of the younger man—that had a black, looming weight of long accumulation, and if it fell upon him, would fall with the vigorous force of youth. Chasing her was love changed, as she thought, to hate; trust to contempt; faith outraged; pride shattered; a man bitterly pursuing a woman who had been false to him; a worthy husband, an unworthy wife: and besides this, the companion of this pursuit was the person whom she would least wish to encounter as the representative of that public scorn she had desperately fled to escape. All this stole the bloom and freshness from the cheeks of the late wife of Mr. Budlong; her flourishing days were past; her withering days had come; and, alas! for her there would be no second spring to follow winter.

Flight is fleet by night and day. Ways of dashing speed traverse half the continent. Flight is independent and baffling with labyrinthine choices. Pursuit must slowly seize its clew and follow cautiously.

In the early confidences of their departure, Belden had learnt the extent of his partner's resources—the twenty-three thousand dollars, profits of Mr. Budlong's summer toils.

"A neat capital," thought Belden, "for a new country. When I get hold of it, I'll let her slide, and after this blows over, I can buy back into society."

So he made for the West, hiding his trail and covering his campfires. But a coward dread permanently overcame him, and he often felt with trembling fingers for his pistol and started when coachmen pointed at him with threatening whips of would-be invitation, or hotel clerks asked his name.

All penal laws are founded upon vengeance. The passion of revenge is necessary for protection. But it is ugly, like the crimes and wrongs that awake it. Mr. Waddy, sternly intent upon the punishment of a scoundrel, whom society could not fully punish, repelled all softer thoughts. He concentrated the whole ire of his nature on this one object. He would not think tenderly of his old love, perhaps still his faithful love. He forgave her for the wrong of his exile, for her imagined falseness: it was inevitable. But what she had become; whether she still remembered him with loving bitterness, with sorrowful despair of disappointed love like his own—this he knew not, would not think of. He would not perplex himself with tender uncertainties.

"Vengeance, vengeance," said his fifteen dreary years. But would she, if she still remembered him kindly, receive him to the old friendship if he came with blood on his hands? He swept away the thought; he saw before him a duty to society.

On, on, silent pair! wronged husband, wronged lover. On, deadly thoughts! voiceless purposes! Fate goes with you and Vengeance and Death!

An ugly muddy ditch, the Mississippi, divides our continent with its perpendicular line of utility. It is not a stream that one used to vivifying seaside waters, or the clear sparkle of New England brooks, would wish to drown in, if drowning was his choice.

The vehicles that run upon this muddy pathway are worthy of its ugliness. At night, majestical moving illuminations, by day they are structures of many-tiered deformity. One of these monsters, a favourite, *Spitfire No. 5*, was to start one sultry afternoon of this same September for up the river. *Spitfire No. 5* wore over her pilot-house the gilded elk-horns of victory; all the passengers were sure of being speedily borne to their destination.

As the boat backed out into the stream and hung there a moment motionless, two men, who had been a little belated in searching for someone they wished to find at the different hotels, pushed off in a row-boat and overtook the steamer. The strong current drifted them out of their course and they boarded the boat unobserved, on her starboard side, away from the town.

Mr. Saunders and his lady, a handsome but rather faded person, had remained in their stateroom until the *Spitfire* was fairly out in the stream. The rail was not yet put up at the forward gangway, and Mr. Saunders stood there, looking at the crowded levee and its hundred monster steamboats, including *Spitfires* from 1 to 10. He was in a moment's pause between two journeys. One long journey was over; another was about to begin. How long he could not say; voyages on Mississippi steamboats may be short, may be lingering. All voyages are uncertain. Fatal accidents often happen. Mr. Saunders, so he entered his name on the books, was just beginning a journey of unknown length.

A greenish gardener from near Boston, emigrating to Iowa, who thought he had seen Mr. Saunders somewhere before, was a little frightened at that gentleman's brutal reply to an innocent question, and observing him nervously fingering at something like a cocked pistol in his breast pocket, shrank back.

"A border ruffian,—perhaps Atchison or Titus," he said to himself, and thanked his stars for his fortunate escape.

The two belated passengers had tumbled in astern and now came forward, with carpet-bag in hand, to ascend the staircase to the saloon. As they passed the gangway, still open, the man with the cocked pistol turned, and they met face to face.

They dropped their luggage and stepped toward him. But he was too quick for them. The nervous, trembling fingers clutched at the cocked pistol; there was a report; he staggered back with his hand at his breast and fell through the open gangway. The great wheel smote upon the muddy current and tossed up carelessly in the turbid foam behind a dead man, with forehead mangled by a paddle-stroke—a dead man, going on a voyage of unknown length along the busy river.

Among the people who rushed aft at the cry of horror that arose was the woman registered as the lady of Mr. Saunders. She saw the body come whirling slowly by and lazily drown away. She sank upon a seat, and was there still in stony, speechless dread, when she felt a hand laid not unkindly on her shoulder.

"Betty, we meant to kill him," said Mr. Budlong; "perhaps it would have been murder. We were spared the final crime. I'm sorry for you, Betty, and forgive you from my heart," and the poor old gentleman, worn out, heartbroken, his life no longer sustained by the tense vigour of a single purpose—poor old Bud drooped and fell blasted, a paralytic, at the feet of his unfaithful wife.

CHAPTER XXIV
MR. WADDY ACCOMPLISHES HIS RETURN

OPPOSITE Mr. Belden's house, which, about the time of his departure from Newport, passed into the hands of his creditors, was the old country place of the Janeway family. It was still in the possession of the representative of that family, under a different name.

The late Mr. Janeway, though a proud and, as it finally appeared, a bad man, remembered the inherited debt of his family to the Waddys, and felt some aristocratic vanity in his tutelage of the young Ira, our hero. A close intimacy of childish friendship grew up between Mr. Janeway's only child and daughter, Mary, and his young protégé. Young Horace Belden, the handsome son of the next neighbour, Mr. Belden, the great merchant, was also a companion of Miss Janeway; in fact, the parents of these two destined them for each other. Adjoining estates, large fortunes, good blood, beauty on both sides—the two fathers thought the match a perfect one and the young people were taught to consider it settled. Something unsettled it. Horace Belden unsettled it by being himself and that self was, from early years, not a noble one. He unsettled it in the mind of Mrs. Janeway, as he grew older, by what he called his flirtation with Sally Bishop, a flaunting girl, daughter of Mr. Janeway's ex-coachman.

Belden, however, remained very devoted to Miss Janeway. He loved her as much as was in his nature, and his pride was fully engaged in winning her, the great match of the day and his by long convention. As he grew older and no better, he began to consider this pure young lady as his bond to purer life and mentally to throw on her the responsibility of his future intended reformation. She must become his, or he would revenge his disappointment, his wounded pride, and his failure of her help and control in his proposed change of character, upon her, upon society, and upon himself.

It was about this time that Mr. Janeway began to discover that too great an intimacy was growing up between his protégé, Ira Waddy, and his daughter. It was well enough while they were children, but the son of a shopkeeper of Dullish Court, and clerk in the counting-house of Belden & Co., was not for Miss Janeway, beauty, aristocrat, heiress, belle. So Mr. Janeway was very distant to Ira Waddy, now a handsome, high-spirited, quick-tempered, energetic young man, full of generous candour and kindliness and gratitude to all the Janeways for the happy and refining influences of their society and their world. The ladies always took Ira's part, but this only confirmed Mr. Janeway in his purpose of making him uncomfortable. At last, this gentleman, finding one day Ira tête-à-tête with Mary, quarrelled with him openly, and finally forbade him the house, speaking very ill of his character.

It may have been too late. Whatever had passed between Ira and Miss Janeway that might fitly be known, Belden knew. Ira Waddy, trustful as he was true, had given his unreserved confidence to Belden, friend of the lady and of him.

Miss Janeway was twenty, two years younger than Ira Waddy, when he, suddenly, one July, fifteen years before this Return of his, went off to those regions where his namesake river rolls. Five years after, the crash in her father's fortunes came. He became an utterly dishonoured man, financially, morally. He could bear his guilt; not its discovery. He died, as it was best he should. His daughter, belle and reputed heiress, did as scores of young ladies of New England have done: she became a teacher in a school and at last a governess. By-and-by, an old lover of Mrs. Janeway arrived. His constancy and devotion through ill-report touched the lady, and she consented to share her distress and her poverty with his humble fortunes at the West. They did not long remain humble. Where he owned a farm, there a town sprouted; where a lot, thither came a railroad demanding a station. His hillsides became stone quarries; his fields, coal mines. His wealth swelled like a fungus of the forest. His wife died and he soon followed her, fairly bullied out of existence by his own stupendous success. His whole property he bequeathed to his step-daughter on the one condition of a change of name. He thus, as it were, ceased to be childless and avoided contributing to the prosperity of his former rival's family.

Miss Mary Janeway, the governess of Clara and Diana and Julia Wilkes, became Miss Mary Sullivan, the woman of fortune. She repurchased the Janeway estate, the house where her happy youth had passed, and it was there she had received Diana.

Mrs. Cecilia Tootler, in combination with Miss Sullivan, managed the charities of their neighbourhood. Miss Sullivan, having no incumbrance of a Thomas Tootler and Cecilia, junior, could superintend also those preventive charities, the schools, utilising here her own experience. In the sick-room or the home of the poor, the sorrowful, or the guilty, these two ladies made themselves welcome. The elder with her deep experience had learnt what others need of wisest sympathy, and the younger came like a gleam of cheerful, untarnished hope.

Cecilia in vain endeavoured to persuade her friend to see Sally Bishop.

"She is dying," said Cecilia. "She is punished for whatever wrong she may have done. But peace of mind is totally denied her. Remorse is killing her faster than her disease. All my consolations are vain. She needs someone better and wiser than I. She needs you."

"Has she asked for me?" said Miss Sullivan.

"No, not to see you," replied Cecilia, "but she speaks of you often with great distress. Do come and see her—perhaps she may have some explanation to give. Mary, Mary, what is this mystery?"

"Dear Cecilia," answered Mary, "it is not because Sally Bishop has been a very bad woman that I avoid her. But she was long ago the willing and exulting means of proving to me not only her own viciousness, but the foul treachery and utterly coarse, detestable baseness of heart and mind of one I trusted as I now trust only God. It was right that I should know the truth, but I must feel a personal horror of a woman whose ill-omened duty it was to tell me to despair and lose my faith and my happiness together. And Sally Bishop did her duty as if it were a privilege and beheld my misery with vile, vulgar, shameless triumph. I abhor the thought of her."

Cecilia said nothing more at the time—indeed, there was nothing she could say. But as the days passed, Sally Bishop grew hopelessly worse, and her father kept himself boozy all the while. Horse-jockeys, pro-slavery judges, gamblers, and collectors of democratic customs sometimes love their families.

Miss Sullivan had just received Clara's summons to Diana's bed of death; she was preparing to go that evening, when Mrs. Tootler drove up in haste.

"Sally Bishop cannot live through the day," said the lady. "She demands to see you. She has a confession to make. Coming death has absolved her from a pledge of wicked secrecy."

And so, by the deathbed, Miss Sullivan, whose best and brightest hopes had been destroyed by the infamy of this poor, dying wretch, listened to her confession and pitied and pardoned her. Sally Bishop, vain and immodest, had nursed in her heart against young Ira Waddy the bitter spite of a shameless woman scorned. Belden, who was her first instructor in shamelessness, discovered this, and used his power to delude her into the joint revenge of the letters. Oh, what carefully villainous letters Belden made of them! how brutally treacherous! how vile! Sally Bishop took the correspondence in Ira Waddy's writing to Miss Janeway.

"There," said she, "you heiress, you great lady, that have stolen away my lover, because you are rich, and are engaged to him without your father's knowledge, see what letters he used to write to me and how he spoke of you and his interviews with you. He ruined me because I loved him, and made of me what you see in my own letters, and I was willing that he should marry you because he always promised that I should be first. But now he is trying to get rid of me. He finds me in the way."

Miss Janeway read the letters as one reads a fascinating tale of horror. There could be no doubt of them; hand, style, circumstances—it was inevitable they were his. Poor, innocent girl—she would afterward see the world and its treacheries, but never any so base as this. Her lover, with her maiden kiss upon his lips—agony! to leave her and write this.

What could she do? Die—and all the lovely sounds of nature that she had learned to love with him from childhood said to her, "die drearily." But it was dreary life that was to be hers and slow-coming patience in her desolate retirement from the world, and experience of domestic shame and shame-crushed life and disgraced death in a darkened household and strict poverty and unaccustomed labour, and by all this a character forming—another woman than the gay, impetuous, proud, loving girl of days flattered by fulness of prosperity. Another in all but loving, and now she must love no more one she could not forget, who had fled when he learnt from her cold letter that his falseness to her was known, she could not sully her pen to tell him how, nor she, a pure woman, hear or speak or think of him more. Love!—what could she ever love again with anything more than quiet interest—she the pale schoolmistress, lonely as that betrothed Mary of the first Ira Waddy, preserver of her grandfather at Bunker Hill?

So this pale schoolmistress was calm and patient and learnt by her own wrong (the only teaching) to hate all wrong and to know it under any specious guise of quietism; and having something much to pardon in her own life, she grew to pardon other ruined lives. She saw how easily sorrow may become despair. A nobler woman she was becoming all these years, but still solitary; loving the many, but lonely of the few to love, until she found in Clara and Diana worthy objects of the closest and tenderest affection.

And now, almost forgetting the wrong this poor dying victim of Belden's villainy had done her, in the sweet pleasure of forgiveness and the dear passion of reviving love, Miss Sullivan must go to the deathbed of her she called daughter, whose sad story she knew. She called Cecilia and resigned to her the dying woman, now at peace.

"I cannot tell you now, dear Cecilia," she said. "I must go. I must think of what I have heard. Only, believe me, she has made me happy, happy again as a child. God forgive her, as I do."

She went to her house by the same paths where her brilliant youth had walked; through the gate where she had so often stood for moments of the shy and lingering tenderness of parting; under the ancient elms whose gracefulness had drooped over her and her exiled lover in many a moonlight of pensive hopefulness. The glory had come back again. The freshness of youth and everlasting springtime was over all the world. She need never again force herself to say that it was good and beautiful; a brightness of transfiguring hope went before her and revealed beneath the drifting away of grey dimness and tearful mists the light of beauty unchangeable and goodness infinite.

Miss Sullivan was to depart on the same journey that Diana had made with such hopeful joy of heart. She had one little act of preparation to do. She took the Testament, her own childish gift, which she had found still the talisman of life to a drowning man, and pressing it very tenderly to her lips, she hung it about her neck. Its touch sent a warm thrill of longing to her fondly waking heart and, with the thrill, a blush shot youth again through her cheeks.

"God willed," she said, "that I who had driven him into exile should be there at his return. How could I not know and feel that one who still in drowning and in death clung to this precious talisman of purest Life, could never be what lies had made me deem him?"

And she went on her journey to be with sorrow and death; but with a joy that no chance of any dying, to-day or to-morrow, could take away. Her joy was of eternity, for she had learnt that love such as hers can never be born and grow and be, unless it is founded upon fullest truth and worthiest worth and most honourable honour in the heart of him she loved—and truth and worth and honour are imperishable and eternal.

In those weeks, while Mr. Waddy was chasing sullenly to overtake revenge, Diana was dying among her tender friends—Clara, forlorn of her noble sister, for whom earth was not found worthy; Dunstan, Endymion, watching, while night after night, the deity of his life and of his heaven fading, perished slowly away until, one violet dawn, she was not. But the sun came up and shone upon his path of manly duty, and he will bravely walk therein, conscious that a beautiful spirit is near him and will never vanish from the sky of his visions.

Ira Waddy was on his return from the West. Revenge had passed away from his heart. He had seen his enemy die horribly, but not by his hand. Death had risen up terribly between him and murder. Merited revenge had overtaken the guilty, but had not chosen him for executioner. And as he turned his face again eastward, he was glad for this—glad that the weight of blood, which he would have assumed unshrinkingly, was spared him. With this storm of deadly-meaning pursuit, with its dark sullenness, unillumined until the final thunder-bolt fell—with this closing crash, all the long accumulating bitterness passed away from Ira Waddy's nature. Heaven was clear and cloudless over him. All mysteries were swept away. It was a new dawn, and a glorious. And he hastened eastward, every moment, long as it seemed, bringing him nearer, nearer——

He had left poor Budlong under the wise and kind protection of Peter Skerrett. And there was another, a woman, who would not leave the old man's bedside, but was there a silent, humble nurse, often bursting into bitter tears, when he inarticulately murmured to her feeble words, which only her quickened ears could construe into intentions of forgiveness.

To arrange Mr. Budlong's affairs at Newport, and his own, Mr. Waddy passed that way on his eastward journey. He arrived, as is usual, in the fresh morning. It was still early autumn, but Vanity Fair had struck its booths, taken down its *étalage*, and gone into winter quarters. The season had ended sadly; everyone was saddened for Diana. Her inspiring beauty had been the brilliant presence that made this summer brighter than any remembered summer. There was many a dry old beau who, stimulated by the thought of her into a brief belief that he could be young, ardent, frank, and brave again, found himself looking with moistened eyes at the places she would illumine no more and feeling that a glory and a hope had passed away.

It would have all seemed rather dreary to Mr. Waddy, walking there alone, but no desolate spot of desert earth is dreary to a man who feels the warmth of his own happiness making gardens sun-shiny, roseate, wherever he treads. Not drearily, then, but full of sad sympathy, Mr. Waddy went toward the house of his gentle kinsman and friend; thinking most of Clara, now so widowed by the death of one dearer than a sister.

"I will ask her who is this Miss Sullivan, whom Granby spoke of as their governess," he said, because his heart was full of gratitude. "Perhaps it may prove that she and my kind friend are one, and I can discover her residence and thank her suitably."

He avoided the main entrance to his kinsman's grounds, and took a narrow, winding path, hedged with rich, close growth of arbor vitæ. At last he reached the house, and passed into the library to wait. As he entered, a graceful figure in black disappeared through another door. She had evidently been sitting solitary reading, for the leaves of a little book on the table were still fluttering. It had a look somehow familiar. Mr. Waddy stepped toward the table and picked it up.

It was his own Testament, gift of childish friendship confirmed by after love, companion of all his better moments, and talisman of safety to his wide-wandering, bewildered life.

He raised the time-worn, tear-worn, wave-worn volume to his lips and, sitting down, covered his face with his hands, and yielded for a moment to the need of happy tears.

He was aroused by a gentle touch upon his shoulder. He turned. It was his old love; his love unforgotten, through all those years of desolate exile, and now—now, his own love forever.

And this was the full Return of Mr. Ira Waddy.

THE END